The Butterfly House

Other books by Valerie Grosvenor Myer

Obstinate Heart: Jane Austen, a biography

Margaret Drabble: A Readers' Guide

Ten Great English Novelists

Culture Shock (a novel)

Charlotte Brontë: Truculent Spirit

Jane Austen

The Butterfly House

a novel

Valerie Grosvenor Myer

Fern House

An original paperback
first published in 1998 by Fern House Publishing
High Street   Haddenham   ELY   Cambridgeshire CB6 3XA

A catalogue record for this book
is available from the British Library

ISBN 0 9524897 2 4

Cover by Chris Winch Design
Ming Dragon by Judith Dale
Printed by The Basingstoke Press (75) Limited

Apart from actual public figures named in the text, no reference is intended to any living person, Chinese or other. Although the events in the political arena described in the narrative actually happened, this is a work of fiction set in an imaginary Chinese university, peopled with imaginary characters. Beijing has forty universities.

This book is dedicated to the students in the Square.

Valerie Grosvenor Myer

1

Jilly Drybrook breathed deeply, listening to the tinkling waterfall, the tropical soundtrack of parakeets and cicadas. Once she idly asked a man who worked there where were the birds of bright plumage, where were the monkeys abseiling down lianas? What wild creatures were kicking up this sweet racket, turning the enclosure into a Prospero's Isle in the middle of suburban London, haunted by the music of equatorial forests? He told her what she already knew, but childishly hoped wasn't the truth, that it was an audiotape, to fool visitors – and perhaps for all anybody knew the butterflies, whose gilded cage the artificial paradise was – into believing they really were in the jungle. It was a miniature and sanitized jungle, without snakes, mosquitoes or leeches, but with a glass roof, reinforced with wire mesh, and neat gravel paths. The butterflies, in their model village, probably knew no better: great four-inch flutterers from South America swooped about like bats, blazing with tropical scarlet, deep violet and peacock blue. The paying public were warned not to handle these fragile insects, with their iridescent scales and delicate antennae. A food tray held slices of rotting banana, brown like decaying teeth, and deliquescent pineapple. Speckled brown, a huge owl butterfly, with a great, glaring false eye on each wing designed to scare away potential predators, was busy gorging.

The womb is a noisy place: thumping heart, rushing blood, gurgling digestive juices, chugging peristalsis, in the humming factory of the human body. Lambs and human children while still *in utero* preferred, according to experimental evidence, Mozart to heavy metal. Who could blame them? I come here to get back to the womb, she said to herself: this is my chosen retreat, warm, a gently humid biospheric environment, with trees and water and artfully winding paths, cultivated wilderness, the compound tiny, convolutions creating a maze.

She reached the enclosure for British butterflies, where common weeds had been planted and cherished, but among those thistles and nettles there didn't seem to be many British butterflies about. *Psyche*, the Greek for butterfly, the Greek for soul. Did the butterflies know they were in prison? What use was freedom, without food, warmth and shelter? Did a modern materialist believe, wondered Jilly, in the soul? The Communists sought to harness spiritual energy to Party loyalty.

'I loved the Party,' Professor Zhang once said mournfully to Jilly. 'But I was criticized for speaking truth and sent to the countryside to be re-educated.' Re-education for Professor Zhang had meant work in the fields, carrying two buckets of liquid manure on a shoulder pole. This called for a tripping step, or the buckets would not balance. 'Very tiring,' Zhang had said. Now Zhang was rehabilitated and had her teaching job back. She had invited Jilly to work in China as a teacher of English.

Another notice told Jilly that the buddleia which attracted butterflies to her patch of garden in Isleworth was the food of adult butterflies, but that caterpillars needed stinging nettles to live on. Jilly's garden was tiny, with no room for nettles. Anyway, there was a small patch of wild ground not far away, bordering a small tributary of the Thames. The district was being redeveloped – overdeveloped, some people said – and prices were rocketing. Everybody told Jilly that her house must be worth a fortune, but she needed it to live in and anywhere else would cost even more. It was small, terraced, two bedrooms and a boxroom, with a narrow hallway, the house she and Robert had struggled to buy when they married, a quarter-century ago, for six thousand pounds. Teeth picked out of his lungs after the accident. Jilly watched the caterpillar on the leaf. Repeats to thee thy mother's grief. Something had been chewing the leaves of her plants into fretwork, and she suspected caterpillars. No butterflies without caterpillars, no grown-ups without labour pains, nappies, vomit, cut knees, adolescent rebellion.

Garden pests had at one time been kept down, Jilly believed, by a hedgehog, but it had been flattened by passing traffic and now, it seemed, none of her plants escaped. Too squeamish to lay down slug pellets, although she was assured they were harmless to the cats who used her garden as a lavatory and scratched up her bulbs, she had laid ecological slug traps: unwashed jam jars, half filled with water and buried up to their rims in soil, drowned the slugs. A nasty method of execution, like burying an enemy up to the neck in sand and leaving him to die of thirst...jars of boiling oil...Professor Zhang said that Chiang Kai-Chek, Britain's friend and ally with a Christian wife, had boiled Communists alive. Or you could put salt on slugs and watch them fizz to death. Warfare over food, eating and being eaten, that's nature. Even Buddhists eat vegetables. Zhang said religion was now once more permitted in the People's Republic of China.

The butterfly house was where Jilly did her thinking. She imagined nuns must feel the same way about their convent chapels.

'I'm a *latchkey* child,' moaned Clytemnestra endlessly, enjoying the expression. 'Why can't you be like Mary's mother, at home all the time?'

'Mary's mother has a husband,' snapped Jilly. 'She doesn't have to keep herself and Mary. She doesn't need to work.'

'She does work! She knits sweaters at home so Mary can go to the convent. Why can't I go there? Mary doesn't see me any more. I hate my school. They call me a swot and say I'm posh. It's not fair.'

'You know perfectly well I can't afford school fees,' said Jilly wearily. In a class full of children whose parents were separated, divorced or not married at all, Clytie played the orphan card relentlessly. Jilly's own father had come back from the war after four years as a prisoner, a stranger. Unable to recognize him, she had resented an interloper and treated him with suspicion. Clytemnestra blamed her mother for everything. Jilly was her own handyperson: she had to be. She painted, papered, did bits of carpentry even. Clytie, sulking, announced as she watched her mother struggling with wallpaper, already pasted and sticking to itself, needing to be forcibly unstuck and ending up crumpled and useless, that Jilly was ridiculous and that she, Clytie, would see she had things done for her. 'You just want to be an ornament, my girl,' snapped Jilly, wiping sticky hands on her jeans, while her beautiful bone idle daughter jeered. 'I've spoiled you.'

'Spoiled? I've *never* had *anything* I wanted,' retorted Clytie in what Jilly liked to call her 'tragedy queen mode'. If only, Jilly sighed, she could have said, as her own mother had done: 'Just you wait till your father gets home.' Jilly had been afraid of her father. Her parents had been disciplinarians, operating a reign of terror. Jilly wondered how on earth it had been done. What was to blame – the generation gap, a changed social climate, or being a single parent? Clytemnestra grumbled because her mother did not keep sweet biscuits in the house. Jilly could not afford biscuits, but to Clytemnestra's disgust smoked cigarettes. Clytemnestra, ashamed of having only a black and white television set, sneered that Jilly was merely stingy. Jilly expected her daughter to praise her for doing so much on so little, to be proud and grateful to her plucky little mother, who barely reached Clytemnestra's shoulder, for doing so wonderfully well, for knitting sweaters Clytie refused to wear. Clytie treated Jilly's efforts with contempt and between dropping out of university and her marriage to Charles had lived on benefits, manipulating the system. Clytie despised money. Even more, she despised those who had not got any for not having it. She told her mother, accurately, that her classmates rode in taxis and ran up telephone bills. Clytie was allowed to receive telephone calls but was not supposed to make them. She whined and screamed that she was an outcast. Clytie bought an old satin jacket for almost nothing and patiently embroidered it with her own design of flowers and butterflies.Claiming that she had no friends, she went to parties in clothes made by herself out of scraps, cursing because she had no dress allowance, and looking exquisite, far more beautiful than I ever was, reflected Jilly, with Robert's delicate bones, his silky black hair.

After Robert's death, Jilly haunted a clergyman who was committed to non-directional counselling. He did not believe in the Resurrection, but did believe in what he called the integration of the personality. The Revd David Loveday revelled in the poetry of Gerard Manley Hopkins and had believed he had a mystical communion with nature. On reading in Don Cupitt that nature mysticism was no rare or special gift, he unfrocked himself and tried to become a painter of abstract pictures, while his wife, a teacher of cookery, kept the home fires burning. His pictures did not sell, his wife left him and he trained in marriage guidance, having joined a socialist splinter group, standing on street corners at weekends hawking its newspaper. Nobody, not even the Revd David Loveday, spoke of sin any more. Even right and wrong seemed outmoded notions.

Jilly sighed and moved over to the incubation tanks, where she stared at caterpillars and chrysalids. Giant butterflies had giant caterpillars, four and five inches long, camouflaged among the foliage they were munching, bright green like living leaves, dull brown like dead ones. Camouflage was Mother Nature's way of protecting creatures from predators, Jilly's teacher at the village junior school told them. Jilly got into hot water for wondering whether, in that case, predators starved to death. Miss Porter was a Christian vegetarian who believed her vocation was to inspire pupils with the miracles of God's handiwork. Miss Porter said that though *some* people believed we were descended from monkeys (sniff) other people thought the world was only six thousand years old, two thousand from Adam to Moses, two thousand from Moses to Jesus. When a boy asked what about dinosaurs, Miss Porter, who had taught that boy's grandfather, said, well, different people thought differently. Some people thought that losing the British

Empire was a punishment for not going to church. Pupils must make up their own minds. China had five thousand years of civilization.

Jilly watched a butterfly being born. Cautiously, slowly, lingeringly, with pain it emerged, stopping every few seconds to fold damp, delicate wings patiently, in exhaustion. Jilly's daughter had been taken from her, washed and laid in a cot away from the maternity ward, a converted workhouse. It had been some time before she was allowed to hold her own baby. *Brave New World*'s bottled babies, still science fiction at that date, seemed to Jilly a good idea: evolution had taken a wrong turn, confining marsupials to Australasia. Lucky kangaroo, six foot tall, giving birth to a beesized baby, who would climb up her fur unaided to her pouch. Why do we not have pockets on our stomachs, she was thinking. Perhaps birth was a struggle for most creatures, except for fish. Butterfly mothers laid their eggs presumably without after-pains, prolapse or post-natal incontinence.

Today's babies, papooses, seemed placid, unlike their grandparents' generation, sternly banished to the garden in their coachbuilt prams, taught the discipline of isolation. Had the reaction swung too far? Jilly was preoccupied with the cultural pendulum. An agnostic, her agnosticism was Protestant in its assumptions, yet oscillating between admiration for the austerity of whitewashed chapels, the upright heart and pure, and seduction by smells, bells and lace, 'gay religions, full of pomp and gold'.

Politically Jilly was uncommitted and refused to believe Communism could be all bad, though her former employer, Josef, an escapee from Eastern Europe, had no good word to say about it. Jilly wavered between what she herself mocked as 'bleeding heart liberalism' and cynicism. Did a woman have the right to choose or was abortion slaughter of the innocents? Crushed heads and tender little limbs torn from baby trunks were not pleasant images. Rabbits often devoured their young or even reabsorbed them before birth. Zhang had told Jilly of a colleague who had come to Britain to research into radioactivity. A Chinese woman, she was appalled to discover on arrival that she was pregnant: her work would be dangerous to the foetus, and Chinese citizens are forbidden to give birth abroad. Expecting an abortion, she was amazed to find herself refused.

'You got the baby in China,' shrugged the doctor. 'It's no concern of ours.'

'I thought you had a National Health Service!' cried the girl.

'You are a foreigner, not eligible. Try a private clinic.'

'It cost five hundred pounds,' Zhang told Jilly later, 'My salary for a whole year! Of course, we all gave her money. We were astonished. In China, it is so easy to get an abortion. We are encouraged, sometimes forced, if we have a child already, or are not married.'

At fifteen, Clytemnestra had an NHS abortion, arranged in conjunction with her headmistress. She had sulked because she wanted to keep the baby and assured her mother she would look after it. The state would keep her and it in comfort, she said. Jilly called Clytemnestra a little slut. Clytemnestra said a girl she knew was only sixteen and she had a baby *and* her own council flat. Jilly said Clytemnestra ought to be concentrating on her O-levels. Jilly told her pregnant daughter she was too young to be having sex. It wasn't legal. Clytie said sex was no big deal. Jilly had waited until she was safely engaged.

'It's not fair,' was Clytie's war-cry. Stuffing her long black hair into her mouth, she rocked on the window-seat, a romantic icon of grief.

'For God's sake, what grudge have you got against the world? Why is nothing ever right for you? I wish I'd never had children!'

'I hate you, too.'

'I'm worn out trying to make ends meet and you won't lift a finger, just keep whingeing all the time. You make me sick, you rotten little bitch. Why have you such a negative attitude? Where's your motivation?'

And so forth. Staring into the glass tank, pullulating with insect life, Jilly saw a slim girl in a white summer dress standing behind her and reflected in the glass. Jilly was visited by the ghost of her daughter, an ivory statue in her wedding dress, reflected in the glass partition of the non-denominational community centre where the wedding was celebrated, for Clytie the rebel had insisted on a conventional wedding. Charles and his best man had even put on morning dress. Clytie, after some tiff with Charles during the cutting of the cake, had flounced behind a tinted glass screen. The girl in the white summer dress moved away. Lucky or not to see the new moon through glass? Jilly could not remember. Suppose the earth were a giant observation tank for unimagined gods to watch us? Jilly was watching leaf-cutter ants building their nests. An ant busily munched a perfect semicircle from the edge of cabbage leaf, using powerful mandibles like an electric saw. Messengers ran deedily with the chopped-up sections along the two-yard log and back again along the one underneath the rotting stump where the circular route began. They didn't seem clever enough to just crawl down the side of the stump and save themselves the journey. Wild leaf-cutter ants used trails over three miles long. Running as fast as their little legs could twinkle, they reminded Jilly of herself loaded with shopping, running for a bus. Ant or sluggard, which was wiser, toiling masses planting rice, gentle scholar Zhang among them, or hippies in the sixties, taking life easy? Ants behaved as if time were money, for all the world as if their rotting log was New York or the Tokyo stock exchange. Man's time a moment and a point his space.

In London, where Jilly was, it was 11 am; in Beijing, whither Professor Zhang had returned, it was 7 pm. Slender men on pedicarts were straining and sweating on their way home, pedalling strenuously to shift weighty loads from one part of the city to another, three-piece suites tied on with rope, flattened cardboard boxes, mixed garbage, quilled like porcupines with plastic Pepsi bottles. Men on bicycles precariously balanced rolls of linoleum on their shoulders. Pedicarts are versatile. Bamboo shelves serve as load-bearing space, as display space, as couch for a snooze or as a stretcher. Endlessly men stripped to the waist, one cotton trouser leg rolled up to avoid being caught in their heavy bicycle chains, toil through the grid of Beijing streets on circular journeys.

Work: the curse of Adam? Ants with the Protestant ethic? Work as identity. Jilly was a supply teacher, a job she hated, her real work in publishing having collapsed. Providence, whatever Miss Porter had told her pupils, offered the worm no protection against the early bird, the small firm against the asset-stripping conglomerate.

Jilly reached the funnel-web spider lurking in her cave, a web of her own skilled weaving above her. Allegedly docile, black hairy monster, obscene female emblem with a poison kiss, a Medusa, she was terrifying. Did she eat her lovers? Here was the notorious praying mantis, three inches long, bright green, a feminist revenge, chewing her mate's head off after extracting his genetic material and perhaps pleasure. Some male spiders wrapped something nice to eat in a parcel of silk and presented it to the female before sex (dinner first). Some crafty fellows, though, wound up an *empty* parcel, and gave it to the lady with a flourish. While she unwrapped the barmecide gift the male sneaked in behind and had her. Josef had been like that. Rumour said he had died in bed with a woman not his wife. Probably where Josef came from mistresses were still an accessory, customary and traditional, like wood-burning stoves and tea drunk from a glass. Jewels, furs, carriages? In nineteenth-century novels, perhaps. She was glad she had two-timed him once at a book fair. But the sexual revolution, like the economic boom everybody talked of, had passed Jilly by. She was ashamed of having had only three men when other women, power-suited and highly-paid, were apparently sleeping their way to the top and having fun at the same time, with children as a bonus. Jilly wore Laura Ashley and a wash-and-leave perm. Josef had frequently told Jilly how generous he was to employ her, but he never took her out, for fear of scandal. Robert had worked for Josef and after Robert's death Josef had taken her over as his responsibility, letting it be understood that as Robert had been a high flyer Jilly must not expect as high a salary. He took Jilly's sexual compliance for granted.

Here was a beautiful green spider with creamy freckles on her body and eight legs. A two-legged featherless acolyte carefully opened the zip on the mesh at the side of her tank and offered her a juicy live bluebottle, placing it delicately on the web, to fool the spider into thinking she had caught it herself. The spider was fed at another's expense, like a kept woman. Josef had not paid the mortgage but he had paid the modest salary which did. Sexual behaviour a social construct, rats and monkeys, even men had to learn how. 'Suffer, bitch!' screamed the flea as he raped the elephant. Jilly wondered whether she had ever had an orgasm. She had heard a woman on radio saying. 'My first orgasm literally blew my head off,' which merely added to Jilly's bewilderment.

'Bit rough on the bluebottle, isn't it?' Jilly murmured.

'Oh, the spider's a new arrival from South America. We're helping her to settle down. Wouldn't do if she went off her feed.' Clytie had been anorexic.

Jilly went to the scorpions, big black armoured brutes six inches long. Full of scorpions is my mind. Then the locusts, whose jaws were even busier than those of the leaf-cutter ants. The locusts seemed unhappy, flying aimlessly about, cracking against the sides of their glass box, their destructive potential confined, like Napoleon's on St Helena. Two inches long, they coupled in mechanical frenzy, in orgies piled three high, dropping off exhausted. Perhaps it was their version of safe sex, like the old custom of bundling? They stared with glazed eyes at Jilly the voyeur. Clytemnestra at fourteen had come home early from school, with a period pain, and found Jilly in bed with Josef. When Jilly was at grammar school, you were supposed to grin and bear it, do gym, play hockey, no excuses. If you suffered, it was your own fault for rejecting your womanhood. Now they let girls loose to come home and find their mothers in bed with their bosses.

The abortion crisis over, Clytemnestra passed her A-levels and went to Leeds University to read history, having been rejected by Durham, her parents' university. After a few weeks she complained Leeds was institutional, shaved her head and became a Buddhist before having a breakdown. In the mental hospital she met Charles, son of a classics don. Charles was interested in animals and growing things but, as his parents constantly told him, he'd never get the grades to be a vet. He suggested he might go to horticultural college but his parents said it wasn't a proper career. They sent him to study chemistry at university. Everybody knew in the early eighties that now so few schools offered Greek or Latin and fewer and fewer students applied to read classics, only scientific subjects led to a secure future. Charles would have preferred to read biology but his parents felt biology was a soft subject and chemistry more reliable, not to say respectable. At the end of his first year he dropped out. After a spell in the funny farm, he got a job in the city parks department as a gardener. Jilly hoped he was happier. The post was not well paid but brought accommodation with it. God knows how it will all work out, thought Jilly, as she walked out of the butterfly house and down the drive. All over the world the females of various species were busy giving birth, feeding and nurturing young, tidying their nests, that unpaid cleaning and maintenance work that holds the world together. What sort of housewife would Clytie make? Would she and Charles be happy together? Clytie's resentments included being kept from her father's cremation ; she grieved that his ashes had been scattered.

'But you were only six, just a baby!'

'He was my daddy, and I loved him.'

Robert had driven out into the night after a row. Jilly had given Clytie a quick slap for some trifling disobedience. Robert gathered his howling daughter up in his arms, on to his shoulder. Jilly, exhausted, screamed at him for taking the child's part against her. Clytie was becoming a spoilt brat, all Robert's fault. Shouts, screams, a smashed cup, smashed car against lamp-post on wet road, corner taken too fast, seatbelt not done up, head through windscreen, teeth scattered, some found in lungs.

2

Was it a cuckoo, that fat dusty bird perched on the garden fence? No, surely cuckoos were shy and grey and she hadn't heard one for years. This was a young female blackbird, sole survivor of the year's second family. Blinking, her mother, broody again, was fluffing her breast feathers over lumps in the soil which she imagined were a clutch of eggs, while the father rushed about finding worms to pop into the youngster's ever-open beak. After depositing each juicy wriggler into her gaping maw, he raced off, running not flying, in search of the next. Law of nature for the male to provide but no, bats, apparently, deserted mothers all, organized a female collective to rear their young. Clytie's voice: 'Why don't we have a car like everybody else?'

'Because your father smashed it up and himself with it.'

What happened to blackbird families if the father fell prey to a marauding cat? Would the female stand on her own clawed feet or would the nestlings starve? Human youngsters were protected, thought Jilly, from the savagery of nature. A few years ago Clytie had saved up to buy a make-up kit, a nightmare amusement: detachable plastic scars, carbuncles, scabs and pustules, livid welts. Children could flirt with mimic disease and death, watching horror videos while sucking sweets in the comfort of their own bedrooms. A poster in the local video shop leered: 'Enough blood and guts to fill an abattoir. An absolute scream! Kiss your nerves goodbye.' Bloodshot eyes glaring from green corpse faces, bloodspattered floorboards, a skull sprouting leathern wings. Who was the artist? Presumably after a day's work he, like the slaughterman or the torturer, took off stained overalls and scrubbed his hands before supper with his wife and children. Jilly in her country childhood had watched the pig being killed every year. It screamed as its throat was cut. Jilly, in rural Gloucestershire in the forties, had carried candles to bed but Clytie, whose grandparents were dead, refused to believe Jilly's tales and accused her of having read too much Thomas Hardy. Pig-killing was functional, not an entertainment. Bloodshed in primitive communities and countries less stable than our own was not a perverse amusement but an everyday reality, along with leprosy, blindness, AIDS and starvation. Smallpox eradicated, but lurking in a glass bottle somewhere, she believed, as a possible retaliation against germ warfare, though retaliation was unlikely to be much use. Clytie had been inoculated against measles and mumps. A pampered generation. Clytie had no idea how lucky she was. A son might have been more understanding. Catching sight of young men, strangers, Jilly often thought, that might have been my son, if he hadn't died inside me. That first pregnancy had turned Jilly into a walking coffin and the second had felt like demonic possession. When the six-pound girl, not clawed and winged as her mother had imagined, but a jaundiced changeling, tore her way out, she rejected the world. Infant Clytie spat out everything except breast-milk and there was not enough of it. Bleeding nipples made Jilly give up and to her shame Clytie failed to gain weight on the various formula feeds she grudgingly accepted in the end. Not my fault. When Clytie became pregnant at an age when sexual intercourse was illegal, Jilly ranted about gymslip mothers. 'I've never seen a gymslip,' retorted Clytie. 'If I have the baby I'll get a council flat.' At the family therapy sessions Jilly attended for a while but which she gave up, being too busy, Clytie screamed at her: 'You were jealous, you undermined me, you forced me back to childhood.' Psychobabble. How could Jilly have put up with a bastard grandchild? Professor Zhang told Jilly there were no bastards in China, thanks to abortion, and no homosexuals either. She had been very curious about homosexuality and asked Jilly endless questions as to what they did. She also asked Jilly to teach her the rude words.

'Why do I spend so much time brooding on Clytie? She's got her council flat and a man to take care of her,' Jilly said to her college friend Rosalind. Though what sort of provider Charles would turn out to be, Jilly was uncertain.

'She's grown up now,' said Rosalind. 'Tell me about this jammy job you've landed.'

Rosalind was lean and dark, with big bright eyes and delicate skin, faintly worn. Like Jilly, she was forty something, still a beauty though growing haggard. She veered between power dressing and shaggy ethnic clothes, barbaric jewellery, embroideries, scraps of mirror glass, like a rich gipsy. Her eyes were ringed with charcoal. She urged Jilly to brighten up her 'earth mother' look with better clothes ('it's an investment') and make-up, which Jilly rarely used. Jilly warmed herself at the fire of Rosalind's vitality. They sat in Rosalind's poky but central flat, full of shawls and bric-a-brac.

'So you met this Chinese woman when you were still in publishing? What sort of person is she?'

'Remarkable. She turned up with an autobiography about the Cultural Revolution and Josef liked it, being a refugee from a Communist country himself, but after he died the new people scrapped it, the way they do. The Chinese government don't let many people out of the country but she came out as a consolation prize for her wasted time in the countryside. I was working on her book and we became friends. She's given me a year's work in her university, to help with China's modernization.'

'Modernization?'

'Means teaching them English so they can catch up with science and trade. She told me that under Mao it was an offence to speak or even to read English. Her father was a professor and they spoke English at home for practice. On his deathbed, in the early seventies, when Mao was still alive, her father said goodbye to his children in English as a final act of defiance. They had a hard time: persecuted as "stinking intellectuals". Children whose parents had been to university were ostracized as "little rightists". She's amazing and her English is wonderful. The context is missing, of course. She saw a picture of Francis Bacon in doublet and hose and cried, "Ah, modernist painter!" And she once asked me what "survival of the fittest" meant.'

'What courses are you going to teach?' asked Rosalind, who lectured at a former technical college, now a poly, and was anxious about her lack of promotion. She and Jilly had read English together at Durham.

'You may well ask. She says the English novel from Defoe to the present day, all in one year.'

'Does the present day really mean yesterday, you know, Joyce and Lawrence, or Snow and Murdoch, or Bainbridge and Fairbairns? And how can eighteenth- and nineteenth-century English fiction, largely embedded in the assumptions of Protestant Christianity,' said Rosalind, who had started out as a medievalist and was now required to teach 'communications', 'help to modernize Communist China?'

'No idea. She says I shall have a free hand. She says Dickens is very popular in China. But which Dickens?'

'You mean should you go for Dickens the reformer of abuses already obsolescent, or the story-weaver of poetically symbolic webs?' yawned Rosalind, stretching like a cat.

'Dunno. Perhaps *Great Expectations* might fit; they discourage personal ambition. I mustn't talk politics or religion to them, you see.'

'You might do a Laingian analysis of *Little Dorrit* – '

'Knowing what we do about the blacking factory and the Micawberish father, I find *Little Dorrit* corrosive. Not very tactful when so many Chinese people have been sent to prison or the countryside, a kind of prison.'

'Mm. See what you mean. My father got out of Germany in time and became a professor instead of a lampshade,' said Rosalind, looking critically at the toes of her high-heeled boots.

'China's full of walking wounded, survivors of mass murder. And though Flora Finching is comical, the treatment is pretty savage, really.

I can't imagine Chinese students getting Dickens's jokes, can you? And how up-to-date is the English they've learned? *Little Dorrit* can be read as a fable about class struggle,' ventured Jilly hopefully.

'Why not *Hard Times?*'

'Too schematic. No, the Tite Barnacles stifle Doyce's energies, and Mrs Clennam is as blatantly symbolic as Clifford Chatterley, the paralysis of the bourgeoisie and all that...Dickens and Lawrence both lower middle class – '

'Didn't I hear that *Lady Chat* was banned in China?' said Rosalind, who called herself a young fogey, getting up to toast crumpets. '*A Tale of Two Cities?*'

'They've just had a reign of terror of their own,' said Jilly. 'No.'

'You'll just have to test the water when you get there, that's all.'

'She says she wants a traditional course in English literature,' mused Jilly. 'What does she mean?'

'I suspect she means a transcendence of the mundane, some universal solvent that reduces warring discourses to an ethereal realm of "beauty", whatever that may mean,' said Rosalind.

Jilly did not know what Rosalind was talking about but did her best to keep her end up.

'Truth is not necessarily the same as beauty, whatever Keats said,' Jilly murmured. 'I can't really cope with romanticism. Nor with Utopias, either, come to that.'

'Then you won't care for China, I suspect. Wasn't it Lenin who said art was less important than politics?' said Rosalind. 'I expect the grip on the arts in China is like the one the Catholic church had in Europe in the Middle Ages. Tough on heretics. I'm sure China observes the Brezhnev doctrine.'

'The what?'

'The idea that once a country has embraced Marxist-Leninism it must never be allowed to slip back. The disputations of the medieval schoolmen are nothing to the endless revisions and reifications of

Marxism. It's a godless creed with all the disadvantages of a theology and none of the benefits, if you ask me.'

Jilly remembered what Zhang had told her about Chinese people living abroad before the Cultural Revolution. 'We were asked to go home and we did. Mao said "Let a hundred flowers bloom" and asked us to make criticisms. When we did, he accused us of being contaminated with foreign ideas, and punished us,' Zhang had said.

Jilly told this to Rosalind, who said, 'Just like the Fifth Monarchy men.'

'Who?'

Rosalind said, 'In the seventeenth century they clamoured for the Jews to be allowed back into England, yelling for what they called toleration. But all they wanted was to lure us back so they could convert us. You can see why we're nervous.'

'They say religion is tolerated in China now,' said Jilly doubtfully. 'Zhang's cousin spent ten years in prison for being a Roman Catholic.'

'Ugh,' said Rosalind.

'They let her out more than ten years ago,' said Jilly.

'Didn't they pour glue over somebody's hair? Some Westerner?'

'Ages ago,' said Jilly.

'Don't get on the wrong side of them,' said Rosalind.

'Zhang says the students will be like British sixth formers,' said Jilly.

'In that case, they won't know *anything*,' said Rosalind and they exchanged anecdotes of present-day pupil ignorance, finding it soothing: 'Never heard of Nero!' 'Eurydice turned to a pillar of salt!' '1688 – year of the *Armada*, for heaven's sake!'

'Chinese students presumably know even less,' said Jilly. 'Have I bitten off more than I can chew?'

'A job abroad will be a shot in the arm,' said Rosalind. 'A good old sexual stir-up is what you need. Did I tell you I'm having a torrid affair?'

'You usually are,' said Jilly. Rosalind always described her affairs as 'torrid'.

'A new one,' said Rosalind importantly.

'Married?'

'Of course.'

Rosalind had never married. Sometimes she said she was looking for someone like her father, at other times she complained she couldn't find anybody her mother would approve of. Jilly thought, but did not say, that Rosalind seemed a little old to be worried about pleasing her mother. Rosalind apparently enjoyed her 'torrid affairs'. She said she wanted to marry, but Jilly suspected Rosalind was hanging on to her freedom, combining pleasure with independence. She was ambitious, Jilly knew. Did these relationships with married colleagues get in the way of her career, or was she bedding the wrong men, like the film actress in the joke who slept with the writer instead of the director? If Rosalind was still sleeping her way to the top, a joke phrase used by both Jilly and Rosalind when they discussed life-chances, it was taking her long enough to get there.

Jilly's brother-in-law Laurence Drybrook was an actor who toured from school to school. He was skilled at making period costumes out of furnishing fabrics to rich effect. He and Jilly met for lunch. Lolo's conversation was usually restricted to green-room gossip ('My dear, his dresser had never even heard of Ayckbourn!') but now he was worried about Jilly, having heard from Clytie, with whom he got on well, of her plans.

'I can't allow it,' he said solemnly over a pizza.

'What do you mean, allow?'

'After all,' said Lolo, his Adam's apple prominent under his black turtleneck sweater, 'I am the head of the family.'

Jilly burst out laughing. Lolo was single and lived alone.

'China's a terrible place! No services, no hairdressers, make-up forbidden, everybody in navy-blue boiler suits, no fresh vegetables, only fried fishy dumplings to eat, blast furnaces in the back garden and Big Brother. You'll freeze to death in winter, get fungoid infections, scurvy, dysentery, putrid sore throats, malaria, yellow fever, blackwater fever, dengue fever, leprosy, no doctors except barefoot peasants, piles of shit in city streets, no loo paper, no sewers except in Shanghai – '

'Oh, come off it! I'm getting all the jabs, I'll take vitamins with me, and my flat will be centrally heated. A quarter of the world's people live in China and they wear padded clothes in winter. It's a wonderful opportunity.'

'You want to expose yourself to feel what wretches feel, don't you?' said Lolo shrewdly.

Jilly shrugged. At the back of her mind was a feeling that if she could rough it a little in China it might offer Clytie a lesson. Clytie had never had to help feed the animals on cold mornings before her own breakfast as Jilly, a farm child, had. Jilly envied her daughter's comfortable existence. Clytie's moans were nonsense.

'They're puritanical as only dyed-in-the-wool Reds can be. Any sort of affairette and you'll be locked up on steamed buns and water, with compulsory political study. They'll take their revenge on you for the opium wars – '

'Zhang says I'll be loved and respected by colleagues and students alike,' said Jilly.

'They're homophobic and they shoot people, and they imagine AIDS is contagious. Be careful who you have sex with.'

'Listen to the puffed and reckless libertine!' teased Jilly.

'Seriously, though, my dear.'

Zhang's picture of China was rosier than Lolo's. Her latest letter innocently offered a rent-free apartment with 'colour television, bed and beddings'. She told Jilly there was nothing to fear. The crime rate was low and any kind of violence impossible. The horrors of the Cultural Revolution would never be repeated. Now was the age of reform, progress, modernization under the pragmatic guidance of enlightened leader, Deng Xiao Ping.

Another friend was Pam, who taught history at the comprehensive school where Jilly worked on supply. Pam used Dickens and Mayhew as evidence in her mission to convince her pupils of the wickedness of capitalism.

Jilly was inclined to agree with her. 'When I read nineteenth-century condition-of-England novels, about poverty and pollution, I recognize the world I'm living in, and I don't like it.'

'Classic laissez-faire, individualism, the triumph of bourgeois values,' said Pam.

'Oh, come off it, Pam. I'm bourgeois, you're bourgeois. You own a house. You run a car. In Eastern Europe we'd be called Intellectuals.'

'I own the minimum for survival in this rotten society,' said Pam defensively.

A lapsed Catholic, Pam had converted to Marxism at Oxford and become hostile to organized religion. Pam had once sent Jilly a postcard from Italy with the comment that the art was 'too religious for her liking'. Her father was a Civil Servant, her mother a social worker. Pam said she was a member of the working class.

'How's Peter getting on?' asked Jilly.

'Don't see much of him,' admitted Pam. 'He's become a Muslim. He says I only adopted him because of underlying racism. Me! It's all down to that shit I married. Peter never got on with his stepmother or her stuck-up brats. Their father pays their school fees. Has your girl got a job yet?'

'Not as such,' admitted Jilly. 'She puts in time at a charity shop, to keep her benefit.'

'Where are she and wotsisname living?' said Pam.

'Council flat. Block's coming down soon, but meanwhile...'

'God how I envy you, off to a progressive country, one where socialism really works. A shame Mao is dead: now there really was a leader!'

'He shot people, encouraged young people to smash up museums, banished anybody with brains to forced labour on collective farms, shut down all the schools and colleges for five years – some helmsman!'

'He shot as few as possible!'

'How's work going?'

'Dreadful,' said Pam. 'Bloody headmaster's a total fascist. Tried to stop me wearing dungarees to work. I'm hoping to get back next term. I was simply burned out. It was exhaustion, but my doctor insisted I was clinically depressed. I said to him: "How dare you? Just because I'm a woman and middle-aged, you patriarchal bastard, you assume it's all menopausal, don't you?" He said not necessarily and had the gall to suggest a psychiatrist! I said to him: "You mean you want some man to ram the values of this rotten society down my throat and label me maladjusted because I want the system changed?" He suggested a woman psychiatrist and I said: "Female psychotherapists are agents of paternalist oppression, guards in the concentration camp that Britain has built for women." So he offers me anti-depressants! I said to him: "Oh, sure, give me the prescription and I'll go to the chemist and collect the tablets and then I'll bring them back here to you." "What for?" he says, looking surprised. "Because," I said to him, "in my opinion all that tranquillisers and anti-depressants are fit for is to be used as suppositories for the medical profession." You should have seen his face! I find alternative therapy much more useful. Do you know about dowsing? It works. I tell what's good for me to eat by holding this pendulum over the food. If it swings in a circle, then it's all right. If it swings from side to side, there's some additive or chemical that would make me lethargic or bring on one of my migraines. Of course the pendulum doesn't know, but it's the channel through which my conscious mind can recognize what my body is trying to tell me. Animals know instinctively what to eat, don't they? I don't eat protein and carbohydrate at the same meal. Every morning I write out a list of possible foods and listen to what the pendulum tells me about them. It's sensitive to my pulses, my own advance and recoil, my own body electricity, its relation to earth's magnetic field.'

'You'll be believing in horoscopes next!'

'There may be something in them. When you're in China, you might try acupuncture. Too expensive for me, unfortunately. I envy you getting your fare paid!'

'Might be expensive there.'

'Barefoot doctors! They ought to organize study tours for those of us who are in sympathy with what their government is doing. It's not fair!'

'It's not a paradise, you know. Whole families live in one room and I believe meat is rationed.'

Pam grumbled that only the rich could afford to see socialism in action.

'Like Shaw and the Webbs in Russia?' said Jilly, but the irony was lost on Pam, who was putting out one cigarette and lighting another.

Attempting to prepare herself, Jilly went to the Chinese room in the British Museum. Chinese art, bland and feathery calligraphic paintings, looked decorative and meaningless to her. It was high summer and busloads of Japanese in matching cotton hats were marching through after leaders holding flags aloft, bored French schoolchildren filled in questionnaires, British couples dragged fractious children by the hand. A hard-up student, Jilly had been grateful for free entry. Now she thought nostalgically of the character in Virginia Woolf, overwhelmed not so much by the exhibits themselves as by the solitude and silence. Television was filling the galleries and art had been brought to the people. If only the buzzing crowd and its crying children would leave the museum to its ancient peace. Fine socialist you are! Jilly rebuked

herself. Zhang said China was the most crowded place on earth. Jilly
wondered whether she would like it there. But it would be an adventure,
a change and a job.

3

Hundreds of rare butterflies escaped from their home in October 1987. An uprooted tree plunged through the glass ceiling in a freak storm causing damage estimated at £30,000. Fragile and pampered, tropical insects innocently flew to freedom in the raw autumn air and died. Jilly thought of Henry VIII, of monasteries, of politicized Tibetan monks.

A single slate blew off Jilly's roof. Her garden, amazingly, suffered almost no damage. The arbour supporting her miserable grapevine collapsed, but the vine was apparently blighted anyway. She remembered a movie in which Richard Benjamin confessed sheepishly to Carrie Snodgress that the vineyard he had invested all their savings in had developed phylloxera, a disease which sounded too exotic for Isleworth.

In November Jilly prepared her garden for winter, grubbing up weeds from clotted soil with bare hands. In a park on the other side of London her son-in-law Charles, a vegan who refused to wear leather shoes, was sweeping up leaves into a huge mound, carting them off in barrow-loads. So frail, those fragile skeletons of cellulose, yet like snowflakes they added up. How many single hairs made a beard? A noise like leaves, all the dead voices, like sand, like leaves. We blossom and flourish, as leaves on a tree. And wither and perish. Not all her garden rubbish was compostable. Her patch was too small to light a bonfire and anyway her neighbours would complain. Clytie had grizzled about having only sparklers instead of real fireworks. Guy Fawkes, terrorist: good riddance to bad rubbish! Or possibly a hero, a freedom fighter. It all depended on your own starting point. Jilly had read somewhere about an immigrant woman who was delighted when the Festival of Lights fell on November 5. What on earth was the

Festival of Lights? Surely nothing to do with the Festival of Light, a
Christian celebration of chastity or something. What was the woman's
religion – Sikh or Parsee, Moslem or Hindu? In China now, Mao's
widow was in disgrace, but it wasn't clear to Jilly whether people were
allowed to criticize him or only to scapegoat the Gang of Four. People
believed such contradictory things and shed blood in defence of beliefs
which others regarded as crazy. On either side of Jilly's fences were
neat herbaceous borders whose owners disapproved of Jilly's
undisciplined clumps, her attempt at organic gardening. They thought it
was common to grow vegetables in a residential area. Jilly, reared to
believe that only the feckless failed to grow their own vegetables,
struggled with Gro-bags. She dug up the fretted remnants of tomatoes
and a few straggly Michaelmas daisies.

During the rest of the year she managed to get some freelance
proofreading, a great relief after being the recipient of obscene abuse
from disaffected school pupils. She was beginning to understand
Clytie's educational grievances. Jilly had not grasped, before she
returned to teaching, how different a London comprehensive of twelve
hundred was from a quiet country grammar school.

In summer 1988 Jilly went to Scarborough to visit Robert and Lolo's
Aunt Helen, of whom she had always been fond. She treated the trip as
a well-earned seaside holiday – so bracing! For fun, because of course
she believed in nothing of the sort, she went to a fortune-teller. Brassy
curls and a smarmy professional manner, peeking slily at her.

'You married, then, pet?'

'Mm,' said Jilly. She can see my hand, with the ring on it, lying in
front of her on the table; damned if I'll let on I'm a widow.

'Got a good man, have you, love?' enquired the oracle.

'Mm,' lied Jilly. Technique ludicrously transparent.

'Children, have you?' persisted the pythoness, peering irritably up at
Jilly.

'Mm,' said Jilly.

The pseudo-gipsy sighed and shamelessly tried another tack. 'Teacher in the family somewhere, I think?'

'Perhaps,' said Jilly cautiously. Most people had a teacher somewhere in the family, hadn't they? 'Aren't you supposed to be telling me things? All you're doing is asking me questions.'

'Not much help, are you, *dear?*' said the woman angrily.

'No tall, dark strangers?' mocked Jilly. 'No journeys?'

'No need to take the mickey. That'll be two pounds, please.'

'I'm off to China in a couple of months, you know,' said Jilly.

'Now she tells me! It's a good thing not all my customers are like you. Goodbye and don't come back.' Downright sneaky. Hoity-toity bitch.

Jilly put down two pounds with a sarcastic smile and left, irrationally disappointed at the woman's lack of insight.

At the Stephen Joseph Theatre in the Round a new play called *Man of the Moment* was running. Aunt Helen, basking in the reflected glory of her nephew the actor, had developed a keen interest in drama and had once been introduced to Alan Ayckbourn at a civic function. She and Jilly went. The play was about a bank robber living it up on a sunny island who got his come-uppance, trampled to death in the pool by the nanny he'd spitefully mocked. His wife wasn't sorry. Secret hatreds. Rosalind had told Jilly that today's students of English literature always asked why Mr Rochester did not get rid of his mad wife, why Paul Morel's unhappy parents did not divorce. Even today, some people were so stingy they preferred to murder their spouses rather than divide the possessions. Would Jilly's own marriage have survived? Professor Zhang had divorced the peasant husband she had been forced to marry during her exile in the countryside. Zhang had been enchanted by Speakers' Corner, to her a thrilling emblem of freedom. To Jilly it was just boring, a platform for crazies. Zhang had been full of questions about the typical British family. Typical? Lolo was a bachelor, Aunt

Helen and Jilly were widows, Rosalind was a spinster. Yet they were all normal members of society. Suddenly she realized who the fat bank robber reminded her of: it was Josef. Too old to be a good lover, despite his greed for female flesh. Robert had been inexperienced. In her case, definitely not all it was cracked up to be. Rosalind seemed to enjoy it, but kept changing partners. Perhaps variety helped.

Next afternoon after tea Jilly climbed the hill, a pilgrim, to Anne Brontë's grave. Saddest of the three sisters, Anne died a virgin, uncelebrated. Curly-headed children were commanded by their father to stand on either side of her melancholy headstone and ordered to smile. Britain as theme park, crowded museums. What was happening to Jilly's faith in mass education? China, where Communism was apparently working, would surely be bracing, restore her sense of perspective. In China, she hoped, the needs of the individual would be balanced against those of society.

Jilly wandered to the lighthouse, a marine museum. The sky was pale green, streaked rose and gold. Harbour lights a fairyland seen from the pier. Here were secret, startling fish, all British fish, like science fiction, irregular shapes, unexpected colours, brick red, indigo, as if from tropical seas. Mystery, unplumbed, surrounded us. Dusk fell and the lighthouse flashed across the water, good deed in a naughty world, a candle in a window, emblem of civilisation. Christianity the lamp of learning kept alive through the Dark Ages, lead kindly light. Yet the Chinese had their own, independent culture, albeit a heathen one. Jilly bought a short-wave radio so she could listen to the BBC in China. Her house was let to a Japanese couple.

In August 1988 Jilly flew to Beijing in a pressurized metal womb with a litter of hundreds, swinging round the earth away from this precious stone set in a leaden sea to the Middle Kingdom, centre of the world as shown on Chinese maps. Could she have survived the social hurricane that devastated Zhang, uprooted her from a cultured home and set her down to feed swine and eat husks, for the good of her character, as an act of class spite? Had Zhang had a breakdown? Clytie had. Fatherless. Smashed windscreen, broken glass, Oddjob sucked to his death, the luckless astronaut in 2001, floating in the icy void like the butterflies after the shockwave hit their crystal palace. Can't make an omelette without breaking eggs, said the revolutionaries. Bloodshed. Bones broken, not eggshells. Jilly recalled Tom Godwin's story, 'The cold equations', about a girl stowaway on a space ship who had, after explanation that the payload did not include her, to be jettisoned. The planet, too, was overloaded, and China had one quarter of the world's people on one-seventh of the world's habitable surface, a biological time-bomb. She hoped there was no bomb aboard the aircraft.

Not all the butterflies were dead, although their sky had fallen. Some had found shelter in potting sheds, had been tenderly picked up and repatriated, to winter cosily in the warm. Others had the sense to struggle back inside after sampling the harsh real world. Jilly was cheered to learn that the owl butterflies had been too drunk on the natural alcohol of rotten pineapple to notice that their Eden had collapsed. Had they been teetotal, like Jilly's grandparents, the butterflies would have panicked and died, but they had groggily stayed put, sleeping and feeding, unaware of their unlikely salvation.

Human beings in London were sleeping in Cardboard City. On the forecourt of Beijing railway station, whole families were camping with their bedrolls, smoking, spitting, waiting for somebody to employ them as domestic servants. Lacking the fare to go home to the provinces, they were periodically cleared away by young policemen, the People's Liberation Army, but in warm weather they accumulated, like moss, on the paving stones.

Underneath the Jianguomenwai flyover was an unofficial hiring fair. A generous employer in 1988 would pay her cleaning woman one yuan (15 pence) an hour; more usual was the rate of 80 fen (12 pence).

Deformed beggars, in rags, plied their trade along Chang'An Avenue, not far from the Friendship Store for foreigners, full of expensive goods, and a mile or two from TienAnMen Square, in 1987 a place few people outside China had heard of, where the children, all singletons, denied siblings by government decree, and therefore specially precious, were happily flying kites, fantastic dragons and butterflies in the bright sunshine of late summer. Foreigners were warned never to take out their purses to relieve the beggars, for fear they attempted a snatch. There were schemes, but the beggars preferred to set their children to pick pockets. Traders besieged tourists, in the late eighties not numerous, attempting to sell pathetic plastic trinkets, Chinese writing brushes, embroideries. In Suzhou, on China's eastern coast, girls spend three years training at the local art school before starting work on the famous double-sided Suzhou embroidery. Freehand, showing the finest colour discrimination among piles of silk thread lying loose beside them, they stab their needles rapidly in and out, deftly copying enlarged photographs of fluffy kittens and cute puppies or goldfish, reproducing perfectly fine gradations of fur or scales. The work is flawless on both sides. The visitors, imagining this exquisite work is machine-made, wave the hawkers away. Tibetans in colourful woven cloaks and hats sit on the pavement selling mysterious animal parts: horns, claws, umbilical cords, all believed efficacious when ground to powder to make medicine for gout, stomach upsets and impotence. Most magical of medicines is tiger bone. The vendors, so picturesque, dislike being photographed, for they, like tiger bone medicines, are illegal, unlicensed.

Jilly was met at the airport not by her friend Professor Zhang but a stranger called Professor Chong and a girl he introduced as Ming, who would be Jilly's interpreter. Ming, he said, was a very bright young teacher of intensive reading. Help, thought Jilly. Plucking up courage, she asked what that was. Intensive reading was paying close attention to detail and extensive was reading for the gist. It sounded highly technical, different from teaching English secondary pupils. Professor Chong had grey hair, rotten teeth and he chainsmoked without apology. As a reformed smoker herself, Jilly found this unpleasant. Later, on a train, she pointed angrily at a 'No smoking' sign and was laughed at by men who blew smoke in her face.

The car drove into Beijing, a hot dusty city of ramshackle courtyards and tower blocks, small street markets but no visible shops or hotels. There was little motor traffic but the streets were crowded with bicycles. Ming, who spoke fluently, escorted Jilly to her campus flat, comfortable and clean, with kitchen and bathroom. A twin-tub washing machine had instructions in Chinese. Ming showed Jilly how to use it, went shopping with her and said Jilly must get in touch if she had any problems.

'What's your telephone number?' asked Jilly, imagining Ming's living quarters would be like hers. But Ming explained she had no telephone. She lived in Young Teachers' Building, on the sixth floor.

'What do I do if you're not there?'

'One of my room mates will take message.'

'How many room-mates do you have?'

'We are four. When we are students, we are six to a room. Now we are teachers, it is better. Not so crowded.'

Ming handed Jilly her first month's salary in advance, a thick wodge of low-denomination notes. Jilly knew her salary as a foreigner was more than Zhang's as head of department, so heaven knew what pittance Ming, just out of college, was earning. Ming led Jilly to the canteen where four kinds of stew were on offer at a low price. Jilly treated Ming to a meal. Ming said it was a luxury to eat in the foreigners' canteen, something she could not normally afford. Jilly in theory despised instant food fixes, for she had a practical bent, but was addicted to tinned babyfood, bland and reassuring. Now she chewed on boiled garlic, served as a vegetable.

'Most foreigners cook,' said Ming. 'They do not like Chinese food.'

'But Chinese restaurants are very popular in Britain!'

'I should like to go abroad,' sighed Ming. 'But before I can ask permission to study in America, I must teach here five years or pay back my tuition. Perhaps I should marry a foreigner. I am joking. I am patriotic.'

Good as Ming's English was, Jilly could never cure her of saying 'Hi, Mrs Jilly!' when they met. Ming always thought of the first name as the surname, which it was polite to use. This apology for a formal greeting, which Ming imagined to be correct, jarred on Jilly. But she liked Ming. The library card index listed Emily Dickinson immediately after Emily Brontë, Jilly later discovered.

Soon Jilly met her neighbours in the Foreigners' Building. Gloria and Ben were Australians, who taught the Chinese teachers; Francine from Paris taught French. The Australians were highly paid by their home governments. Francine and Alice, an American teaching English, were like Jilly on local salary.

Gloria was sandy-haired with a face like a freckled bas-relief. She lived next door to Jilly and told her that she, Jilly, would never be able to manage. Jilly protested that she earned more than Zhang.

'They're Third World, though,' said Gloria.

'So that's all right, then?'

'Their families help them out,' said Gloria.

'The poor helping the poor?'

'They certainly don't live on what they get paid. Nobody could.'

'They look so shabby,' said Jilly, eyeing Gloria's well-cut trouser suit.

'That's because they salt money away instead of spending it. Don't listen to hard-luck stories. Chinese men aren't any sort of temptation, are they? Rotten lovers, I understand. Girl here last year had a big thing with a Chinese fellow but it all fizzled out. He was all set to go back with her to the States, but the authorities insisted on him marrying somebody else, a Chinese woman, before they'd let him go. He wouldn't consummate the marriage and planned to get a divorce as soon as possible. He made the mistake of telling his Chinese wife and she told the Party and the high-ups made him screw her! His duty to the party. In this sodding country talebearing isn't just a duty, it's a pleasure.'

'How sad!'

'You'll get used to sad stories if you stay here long enough. Just let them get started on what happened during the Cultural Revolution. I loathe the bloody Chinese.'

'Then why are you here?'

'I met an Australian at university in Edinburgh and married him. I'm Scots originally. He went home to do his doctorate and I followed, putting him through, you know, casual work. He got his fucking PhD and then told me he'd met somebody else, also married. So I went back to university and qualified as a teacher of English to foreigners. And the government sent me here.'

'What happened to the girl who was involved with a Chinese man?' asked Jilly.

'Back in the States. They don't like us getting close to the Chinese. That's why, unlike other employers, they prefer middle-aged people – less chance of complications. They really like married couples; these flats are meant for two at least. Two Chinese couples would love to have a flat like this, sharing kitchen and bathroom. They don't like us to hang around here too long: it's all contract work. This is my second year out of three. We soon get disillusioned. What they like here is starry-eyed people, but not too young and not too far left. Had too many Maoists who came here and told them how to run a Communist country. Chinese Marxists look down on Western Marxists as being woolly and unreliable. I'm not very political myself, but I don't care for Communism or Communists. Don't ask anything about the Party: it's considered bad manners. Only Party members are allowed to go abroad, you know, but they're told to deny it. You can't trust anybody. Be very careful. You know you mustn't talk to students about politics or religion, don't you? You wouldn't enjoy being re-educated.'

'Zhang didn't enjoy it, certainly.'

'Oh, hard-luck stories. It'd be worse for you. Time was, all foreign teachers used to live at the Youyi Binguan, the Friendship Hotel. Lovely place, wood floors, fifties furniture, built for the Russians, but they went home in a huff in 1960. So now the Friendship is being refurbished for Japanese sarari-men at high rates and we're all shunted out on to campus. No facilities except the canteen. At the Youyi there are shops, coffee shop, hairdresser, a bar, Western films, tourist information – all the things we do without. Mind you, our flats aren't as bad as some.'

Gloria's was crammed with loot: quilts, embroideries, fans, Chinese paintings, vases, jade, porcelain, Buddhas, feathers, puppets, shawls, camera and lenses, compact disc player, food processor, electric tin-opener, a microwave imported at great expense and plugged in to the living room power point because the kitchen had a gas ring but no electricity, push-button radio and a cordless telephone, dinner service and cutlery.

'Golly, you have got some stuff!' said Jilly.

'It's my *home*,' said Gloria.

'I'm trying to live simply,' said Jilly.

'Whatever for?'

'I don't want to flaunt in front of the Chinese, when I'm so much better off than they are.'

'You'll soon get tired of that,' said Gloria. 'I promise you, you'll never feel guilty about using machines or buying anything wrapped in unnecessary plastic again, when you get away from this place. The sheer inconvenience of life here can drive you crazy.'

'It doesn't seem to drive the Chinese crazy,' said Jilly.

'They never smile,' said Gloria, glumly.

'Perhaps you don't smile at them?'

'We all feel the strain. After about six weeks, you'll feel lethargic if you eat canteen food. Always minuscule quantities of pork with vegetables. There just isn't enough protein. It's such a fiddle to eat that you imagine you're satisfied by the sheer effort of tweezing the bits up with chopsticks and it's only after an hour or two that you realize you haven't eaten enough to be nourished. That's what people mean by being hungry after a Chinese meal. You can't get cheese or butter here easily. Calcium deficiency is a serious problem. Look at all the bad teeth. Fresh milk sells out too fast at the Friendship Store; you can buy unpasteurized milk in plastic bags, but you'll get brucellosis. Mostly I use powdered milk. You can buy proper Western food at the hotels, but that means special trips by taxi because our shopping bus only takes us to the Friendship Store, miles from anywhere.'

'I was planning to live on canteen food,' said Jilly. 'I don't want to be a colonialist, an expat.'

'You'll be ill unless you supplement your diet. I hope you brought vitamins? Oh, good. The world looks different from this side. Britain's not the centre any more: it's all happening in Korea and Japan. Hong Kong is a major money market. Their businessmen are all setting up bases in Singapore and the Caribbean, ready for the handover in 1997.'

'I've heard that Hong Kong is likely to be left alone,' said Jilly. 'Zhang says this country has gone money-mad.'

'Don't overestimate the Chinese capacity for change,' warned Gloria. 'Mao was the last of a long line of emperors, a Communist emperor. Confucian ideas graft easily into Communist ones. Old Deng is doing his best, but the problem now is inflation: prices in the shops went up a hundred per cent last week, and the government had only just announced a price freeze.'

4

At the first meeting for the foreigners Gloria introduced Jilly to the Russian teachers Tanya and Irina. Their English was limited, but they were friendly. Tanya was small and dark, Irina a large blonde. Both were smartly dressed and Jilly wondered whether her smocks and jeans were too casual. A blond young man made a late entrance, without apology. He was wearing a scarlet leather batwing jacket with stone-washed designer jeans and shoes of pale suede, his slim right ankle poised over his left knee. Jilly assumed he was American, as she had heard American men sat like that, and avoided sitting crosslegged for fear of being taken for faggots. Negligent grace, poised vulpine head, expensive haircut, thick dark eyebrows, clear grey eyes, olive skin, dimpled chin, male beauty that made Jilly gasp.

The meeting was chaired by the Waiban, or head of the foreign office, Mr Da Feng. He spoke in Chinese, while Professor Chong translated. Gloria muttered to Jilly, 'Careful what you say when he's around. He can speak English all right when he wants to. Understands more than he lets on.'

Mr Da was good looking, with a charming smile. Jilly wondered whether Gloria might not be unduly cynical. Da warned them that China was a developing country and they must not expect the standard of living they were used to, but he would do his best to see they were comfortable. Problems should be referred to him.

The beautiful young man introduced himself as Fox.

'Surname or Christian name?' demanded Gloria.

Fox smiled, showing perfect teeth.

'I never use my first name,' said Fox. 'We spell it F-A-U-X and the main branch of the family pronounce it Fawkes, like Guy, you know, a distant ancestor, but we in the cadet branch sometimes call ourselves Foe. Chong didn't translate everything Da said, you know.'

'Know Chinese, do you then?' said Gloria.

'Just picked it up here and there. Papa being a diplomat, I went to international schools. Mummy is Spanish and I was actually born in Argentina.'

'What have you been doing so far? Teaching?'

'This and that. Secret work, mainly. I've been with the Sandenistas. Teaching is my cover.'

'If so you've just blown it,' said Gloria. 'I hope you're not one of those boring people who make mysteries out of trifles.'

Jilly thought this rather rude. Fox interested her.

Alice and Jilly were both in the literature department. Alice was a short, plump American woman who dressed like a Chinese in padded jacket, cotton trousers and cotton shoes. Alice said a few words in Chinese to Fox, who failed to understand her.

'I thought you spoke Chinese,' she said.

'A little rusty,' said Fox. 'I was here in 1983. Very different.'

'Absolutely!' cried Alice. 'Prosperity has *rotted* the Chinese character, eroded the traditional virtues.'

'What traditional virtues?' asked Gloria.

'Honesty. Thrift. They've turned greedy. I came here in '84 to learn the language, and everything was so cheap. Now they're asking five cents for a cabbage! You never used to pay more than two. You could buy cashmere sweaters for sixty dollars each; now they're up to two hundred. Mao forbade make-up,' said shiny-faced Alice. 'Now they charge sixty dollars for a box of imported eye-shadow in government stores!'

'A box of eyeshadow?' quavered Jilly.

'Yes,' said Alice, looking virtuous. 'Rich pedlars, mostly; jailbirds. Finished their sentences, but no work unit will accept them, so they're

given a pedlar's licence. The government used to control all buying and
selling.' She sighed,

'You sound sorry,' said Gloria.

'I think it's a shame that the wives and daughters of criminals
should be wearing trashy make-up and flashy clothes.'

'Never mind, Alice. No fear of your showing students a bad
example,' said Gloria.

A banquet welcomed the foreigners, with polite speeches, beer, fizzy
soft drinks and a tasteless white spirit. Gloria said, 'Last year we had
maotai.'

'Costs as much as Black Label now,' said Benedetto, who looked
like a Mafioso, stocky, swarthy, blue-chinned, balding, with pebble
glasses indoors, shades in sunlight. He wore dark suits with roll-neck
sweaters and outdoors usually a soft black hat. His manner was mild,
but reserved.

'What's *maotai* ?' said Jilly.

'Graveyard smell,' said Ben. 'Very strong.'

'Too strong to be good for anybody,' said Alice. 'Nothing sadder
than an alcoholic.'

Gloria murmured to Jilly, 'She used to be a Maoist. Now she's a
Born Again. She just has to be the oldest American virgin in China.'

'How old is she?'

'Dunno.'

Mr Da Feng, life and soul of the party, cried loudly, '*Ganbei*!
Ganbei! No heeltaps!'

'Go easy,' Ben warned Jilly softly. 'He loves to make the foreigners
drunk.'

The party started at five-thirty and broke up after two hours. When
the foreigners, except Alice, tried to make a night of it in the only hotel
anywhere near the university quarter, they were firmly told 'No bar' so
they dispersed.

On Jilly's first morning, she found her classroom locked. Eventually the monitor appeared with the sole key, which he insisted on keeping. She made repeated applications during the year to Mr Da and Professors Chong and Zhang for a duplicate but was refused. The monitor controlled access. She complained when he was late, as he frequently was, and was told she was making a fuss about nothing. Students arrived one at a time, yawning. Zhang, whom Jilly had seen only briefly since coming, had told Jilly her classes would be no larger than twenty. Zhang had not explained that classes tripled up, so that a classroom built to accommodate forty was crammed with sixty bodies. The walls were stained. One window was broken. A table to the right of the old-fashioned teacher's desk held some dusty Gestetner typescript, a battered sports trophy and three stringless badminton rackets. Fluorescent lights did not all work and the wiring looked dangerous. Somebody had removed the top of the power point. Crumpled newspaper littered the floor. Nervous of fire, Jilly insisted that the room be cleared. Reluctantly, the monitors found twig brooms and half-heartedly swept the rubbish into a corner. Sulking, they eventually took it to a bin in the corridor. Her chair was covered in chalk dust and she commanded them to clean it before she sat down.

The classroom was on the fifth floor. Long flights of concrete steps were occasionally cleaned by women who sloshed down buckets of cold water and pushed desultorily with rag mops. Jilly thought of the cascade at Chatsworth. Gloria made constant but futile complaints about getting her feet wet.

'What about my *shoes* ?' she demanded in English of the bewildered peasant girls, illiterate dialect speakers. Even standard Chinese was alien to them. Wisely, they ignored her, knowing all foreigners were mad and too stupid to speak intelligibly.

For all the water-throwing, the teaching building was grimy, and stank of urine. Every so often, Jilly would throw away the useless badminton rackets, but they were always replaced by unseen hands. Not being allowed a key, she was reduced to putting up displays of postcards with Blutak as she talked. Big Ben, Charles and Diana, last year's Christmas cards, all disappeared. Asked who had pinched them, the students just grinned.

In September the trees were musical with cicadas. Bats wheeled at evening and earlier there were big blue dragonflies. Recent battles had left their scars: the walls still bore the faded slogans of the Cultural Revolution, never erased. Red paint drips on the concrete looked like bloodstains. The university was a building site. Workmen in singlets and baggy cotton trousers often sang as they worked with picks and shovels or laid bricks. One would start up and the rest would join in the chorus. Taking a walk round the leafy campus one evening, Jilly met a young man singing a melancholy song, perhaps of battles not so long ago.

Nights were hot. Jilly mentioned to Ben that a mysterious noise, like a creaking window or dripping tap, kept her awake.

'Probably a cricket,' he said. 'They creep into damp places. Want me to have a go at it?'

He came in and bashed away at the pedestal of her basin with a flip-flop sandal. But that night and the next the noise was as bad as ever. One night Jilly hunted in her Chinese pin-yin dictionary and telephoned the guard house, for the foreigners lived in a secure compound. In what she hoped was Chinese she said 'Cricket in my room'. The old man whose duty it was to protect her just grunted. Had she been telling him there was a cricket *team* – in there with her, perhaps?

Next day, Jilly told Ming, who told one of the cleaners. The girl giggled. 'I kill 'em,' she said, surprisingly in English, and reappeared with a spraycan. The cricket was silenced, but others took its place. Soon Jilly got used to them. Cockroaches in her kitchen were different. She decided to ask Ming.

The teachers' dormitory was up dark concrete steps. Ming's room was along a dim, damp corridor festooned with dripping washing, the laundry room bare except for stone sinks with cold taps. Ming's tiny room had four bunk beds and a mosquito net.

Jilly said the mosquitoes troubled her, too. 'They say you can buy electric mosquito killer at Friendship Store,' said Ming. 'Too dear for Chinese.'

The cell was decorated with posters, photographs, soft toys, a portable radio-cassette player and four enamel bowls. The girls cooked on a spirit stove on the bare concrete floor and ate sitting on their beds. Ming confessed to Jilly that cooking was forbidden because of fire risk. 'Cheaper than canteen,' she said. 'Now we are teachers, it is better. We were six to a room. Our dormitory is full. We are lucky to have room. One of the teachers is married and lives in a classroom in the teaching block. They must wash clothes in the toilet.' Jilly understood the wet washing she had seen near her classroom. Feeling guilty about her own comfort, Jilly murmured something about cockroaches.

'They are everywhere,' said Ming. 'You can spray.'

Jilly's brief was to lecture on literature and teach English composition. She borrowed some travel videos from the British Council library, all out of date. She talked to the students about what they had seen and set them to write about their impressions. Her harvest was not what she had hoped for. She learned that Oxford and Cambridge universities were in London, that Middlesex was in South Ontario, 'where seats the world-famous planetarium Greenwich'; that Britain was in the Pacific and 'when two religious holidays comes every years, the whole state is mad for happiness', with 'folk dance, sports, also some pastimes peculiar'. The youth 'longed for going to Oxford and Cambridge to abandon much knowledge'. Personal response of any kind was rare, though Mei Ling, a skinny lad, said to Jilly, 'Your country is so beauti-*ful*, like a gar-*den*.' She was astonished to find that the Chinese students recognized British politicians and their offices: Clytie could never have passed such a test.

Ben was becoming Jilly's mentor. 'I hoped they'd write about what they'd seen,' she told him. 'They were fascinated by bagpipes and kilts, but never wrote a word about them. They just plagiarize.'

'Of course they do. They're trained to listen, memorize and reproduce. When that's too hard, they consult reference books. Your task was too difficult, so they went to Chinese sources and translated them – hours of work. Garbled, but half these kids are from mud-hut villages with semitrained teachers. Expressing themselves in English at all is an enormous achievement. They're not stupid.'

'Their thinking is ahead of their power to express it, but they keep making the same elementary mistakes,' said Jilly. 'They forget plurals and agreements, muddle up nouns and adjectives – '

'Simple interference from the native model,' said Ben. 'Chinese has no plurals, verbs are invariable, adjectives and nouns are interchangeable. How's your Chinese coming along?'

'I take your point,' said Jilly, humbled.

Ben said originality and independence had not been encouraged in China. Obedience and conformity were Confucian virtues. 'Despite inventing gunpowder, the compass, paper and printing, the Chinese didn't achieve the scientific revolution: Europe did, from a lesser start. Chinese who get to America win prizes: don't underestimate their intelligence just because four-fifths of the population are illiterate. You notice how well your students spell in English? They're trained to recognize the shapes of words. Don't ask them to write about Britain: ask them to write in English about their own culture and traditions and you'll be surprised.'

So instead of reading about 'French skyscrapts' and 'ancient Great London bell', both of which puzzled her, Jilly discovered a Chinese English which seemed too poetic to correct. Strong winds from the Mongolian plain brought 'tons of dust like giant knocks his pepperpot over'; the Moon festival 'evoke deep feelings in your bottom'; and she learned that 'Chinese are working-harded bravery clever people'.

Ben suggested to Jilly that she might like to visit the Great Wall one weekend. They got up early, eating pancakes from a breakfast stall, and caught a bus. The mountain scenery was bright pink and purple with dewy convulvulus.

'What's your reason for being here?' asked Ben.

'My daughter got married,' said Jilly at random.

'Are you running away from something or someone?' he asked gently.

'Why should I?'

'Many people use this as an unoriginal substitute for the French Foreign Legion. They come here to lick their wounds, recover from relationships that went wrong, to forget. Forgive me if I say you seem something of a lost soul.'

'Are you married?' Jilly asked.

'No,' said Ben. 'I'm celibate.' He fell silent.

'Why ?' said Jilly.

'I trained as a priest, but I supported Liberation Theology. I haven't broken my vows. My ministry is everywhere and my vocation called me here.'

He responded to the friendly curiosity of the other passengers in Chinese. 'Warmly welcome you to China, they say,' he reported. He did not pass on that the Chinese assumed he and Jilly were married. 'They're afraid we might get lost and keen for us to appreciate the wall. They're convinced it can be seen from the moon, but as the wall isn't as tall as the Pyramids or the Empire State, it must be a folktale.'

Soon on the horizon they glimpsed the crenellated Great Wall itself, cresting the hill like a dinosaur. The coach park was crowded with souvenir stalls.

Ben said to a persistent hawker, '*Wo bu mai, xie xie*,' and the man answered angrily. The word rippled down the hill from stall to stall, '*Neige waiguo ren shuo Zhonguo-hua*, the foreigner speaks Chinese!'

Jilly asked what was happening. 'He said if I wasn't buying I could go back to America, so I told him I was Australian but he didn't like that either.'

Despite threats that graffiti, spitting and 'littering' would be punished, the wall had plenty of messages in plenty of languages. Through the jostling crowds, Ben and Jilly climbed from watchtower to watchtower, looked down on the cars diminished to toy size, out at wild green hills and blue distances, and did not buy 'I climbed the Great Wall' T-shirts. A sign said in English, 'Western fast food, tea, coffee' but their enquiry was met with chants of '*Meiyou cha, meiyou kafei, meiyou hamburber*.' Nothing doing. Eventually they found some canned Coke, extra-sweet. Ben suspected it was new formula stuff, unpopular, so dumped on to the Third World.

'It's a good spiritual exercise to think yourself into Chinese shoes and convert your irritation into compassion,' he said.

The returning bus took them to the Spirit Way, an enchanted path bordered with stone animals, stone warriors and stone sages.

Jilly thanked Ben for his company and did some shopping at the food market near the campus gate. There were no wrappings, not even newspaper, cucumbers wore no condoms, fish swam in tanks and were carried home alive, thrashing on hooks. So were live ducks and chickens, swung by the legs, for freshness is important. Sides of meat were flung down in the gritty lane and dragged into the shop to be cut up. Fat and gristle, most of it was: when Chinese teachers had a party, they asked foreigners to buy meat for them at the Friendship Store, the only shop with an electronic till. Everywhere else people used the abacus. Shop assistants were notoriously surly and seemed to enjoy calling out triumphantly, '*Meiyou!*' Taxis were hard to find and expensive. The foreigners grumbled constantly and Ben gently rebuked them.

Hot water was a problem, available only early morning and late evening. One morning the bathwater was full of mud and rust, chocolate brown. Gloria called a meeting and proposed that unless all-day hot water, which she said had been available all the previous year, was restored, a strike threat should be sent at once to the Waiban, Mr Da.

'It might be more tactful to have a quiet word with him,' said Ben. 'Not a good idea to make him lose face.'

Gloria stuck to her point.

'If you hate everything so much, why are you here?' said Francine.

'I wanted a change. I don't intend to put up with deteriorating conditions –'

'Have you seen the way the Chinese live?'

'Neither here nor there! What I'm saying is – '

'Grossly insensitive to complain,' said Ben. 'These are luxury flats by Chinese standards. Our Chinese colleagues come sightseeing to our stately homes – '

'We're used to living decently – ' said Gloria,

'We are privileged!'

'Don't try to give away my rights!'

Gloria was outvoted and it was agreed to wait a day or two. If the trouble should right itself, no complaint should be made. If the bathwater remained grungy, Ben would, he promised, drop a word in the right ear.

Next morning Jilly was on her way to class when she was stopped by Mr Da, who got off his bicycle.

'Mrs Jilly,' he said reproachfully, 'I hear you complain.'

'No, I've not complained.' The bathwater had been slightly stained that day.

'You went to meeting,' he accused her. He was an attractive man, rumoured to be father of a bastard child. 'You were willing to write letter.'

Sheepishly Jilly admitted it.

'China is developing country,' warned Mr Da. 'We want foreign friends happy. Make trouble is not Chinese way.'

'I don't make trouble,' said Jilly. 'I'm very comfortable and the flat is very nice.' Already she had heard of mouldy walls, falling bathroom tiles and poor heating at other colleges.

'Always Mrs Gloria make trouble,' said Mr Da, and pedalled away.

Suspicion buzzed among the foreigners. How did Mr Da know there had been a meeting?

Alice was convinced all telephone conversations were recorded and transcribed. Gloria thought this would explain everything. Ben laughed. Gloria accused him of sucking up to the Chinese.

'I had a word with one of Mr Da's underlings,' said Francine later.

Gloria said this was underhand.

'Meetings are illegal in China, you see!' she said.

'Paranoia,' said Ben softly.

Francine said she had lived with Chinese people before. 'It is bad form to be angry. If you have a grievance, you do not mention it directly, but discreetly, through a third person.'

Gloria whipped out a photograph she had taken of the chocolate-coloured water.

'If it goes on happening,' she said grimly, 'I've got *evidence*.'

'You realize, of course,' said Francine, 'that Mr Da is under pressure to keep the foreigners happy. If we complain, the Party will criticize him.'

'Oh stuff the Party!' said Gloria.

'That's just what he daren't do,' said Ben. 'What they call criticism is more like excommunication. It's not just a mild ticking-off, you know. It means heavy psychological pressure, practical sanctions. Our contracts, as well as forbidding us to raise poultry indoors, mention the possibility of "re-education" if we are unsatisfactory. I don't think we would enjoy it at all.'

Ming mentioned, whether deliberately or not, to Jilly that because of her own teaching schedule, all the hot water was gone by the time she got to the bath house, where the water was heated for a couple of hours on Fridays. 'Mostly it goes to the foreigners,' said Ming. Jilly invited Ming to use her bathroom, but Ming refused, either from pride or shyness.

Cycling off campus a few days later, Jilly saw a girl living on the city fringes. She was washing herself at an outside tap, splashing her bare arms and legs with cold water. She had no towel.

Later, after her bicycle was stolen, Jilly got used to travel by service bus. People fought to get on and off, flailing elbows, and once on were packed tight. Every gear-change brought a violent lurch. Usually Jilly was the only foreigner on board and strangers approached her to practise their English, always assuming she was American. Children stared at her, amazed at her mousy curls, bleached skin and distorted features. A few wept in terror at the sight of the *waiguo yanguize*, the foreign monster. Jilly smiled bravely at their mothers, who smiled back. She felt she was making some progress.

5

Dear Rosalind,   September 20, 1988

I may have blotted my copybook. If I'm locked up, make
representations to the Foreign Office. I asked my class to write me a
letter about themselves and they groaned that every foreign teacher
asked that and they were sick of it. I learned they all had to spend ten
days in the army before college, so muggins suggested they write about
that. A few did, but others refused. Party activists in the class
disapproved and thought I must be a spy! Seems to have been tough:
not allowed to eat till they'd learned 'orthodoxical revolutionary
songs'. Mei Ling, an interesting boy who is apparently a poet, wrote
that when they arrived, 'Our bright clothes flowered the camp.' Soon
they were all in drab olive. Rats, mice, lizards and flies in the barracks
(oh, I found a little lizard in my living room the other day) but one girl
wrote that despite square-bashing and lessons on how to shoot, they
were 'guarded like goddesses'. The sexes here are strictly segregated
and their development is socially retarded.

Every class has two monitors, one male, the other female. They are
actually class chairmen and have to be Party members, often I
understand a bit thick but ambitious. Despite lipservice to workers,
peasants and soldiers, my young people do not seem keen to work
anywhere except in the cities or abroad, in commerce.

Professor Chong sent me a message: please will I tell my students
all about what he calls deconstructivism. I know nothing about it and
care less and of course without books I can't possibly cope. Chinese
memories are so well trained that people here don't grasp how
dependent we are on reference books.

I watch the Olympics on TV, but as they show only Chinese successes here, I have no idea how the Brits are doing. The air here is very dry, lips cracked, hair like hay.

Write soon. I feel a bit cut off.

Love, Jilly.

Summer weather lasted right through October, season of supervised student parties, ending at nine as smooching in the dark was strictly forbidden. Sweet cakes, melon seeds, apples, soft drinks only, amplified Western pop music with Chinese words, and uninhibited dancing.

'Demonic possession or public onanism,' murmured Ben to nobody in particular.

'Disgraceful,' said Alice. She peered at Jilly, who had put on lipstick and a bright smock. 'My land, you *are* dolled up, aren't you?'

Dumpy Alice was wearing her usual grey tunic and black trousers with cotton shoes, like the old woman who lived by collecting empty aluminium cans, hobbling on three-inch feet. Alice's feet were large. Ming was wearing lipstick and her best blouse. A few girls wore peasant costumes.

'China is proud of minority people,' said Ming. 'They may have two children, even three.' She sighed.

Everybody was expected to do a turn. Students sang, danced, did acrobatics. The Russian ladies sang a duet. Jilly obliged with 'I remember, I remember', which went down well, but not so well as Fox's song in Spanish or Alice's recitation of a poem in Chinese by Li Po.

'I wish I could speak Chinese,' said Jilly to Professor Chong. Zhang was, as usual, busy elsewhere.

'You don't need to. We all speak English. Never have I met a foreigner who succeeded to speak Chinese perfectly. One of our emperors heard a European speaking Chinese and asked his vizier,

"Which traitor taught this stranger our language?" May I tell you of a mistake a foreign friend made? I must warn you, it is vulgar.'

Disliking Chong, who was smoking all over her, she smiled feebly and despised herself.

'The foreigner, an American, made a speech at a banquet. He meant to say he had two homes, one in America, the other in China. But he mistook the tones, so he said, "I have two farts..." The Party, you know, does not like foreigners to ask too many questions.'

Was this a threat? Jilly, sitting on the top table, wondered whether it would be rude to leave. Gloria had, she gathered, given offence by not turning up. Jilly went to her lonely bed and dreamed of celibate Ben.

Dear Rosalind,   October 10, 1988

Last weekend I went into town. For the first time I felt I was in the mysterious East, among alien gods. I went to the lamasery, curly roofs and gold leaf, a Buddha eighteen metres high carved from one cedar trunk. During the Cultural Revolution it was closed down and protected from the Red Guards. Monks here don't work the eight-hour shifts they do in the tourist traps. They have the mild, preoccupied serenity of true contemplatives as they bustle calmly about (if that isn't an oxymoron), lighting candles, burning incense. Brown habits, orange sashes, a bit like Franciscans, shaven heads.

We went across the road to the temple of Confucius, the exam room where candidates for the civil service were locked in for three days. Some died, others went mad. I imagine they counted as failed. Hardly anybody was there. We wandered into a museum I could make little sense of, except for a fresco of Mao on the balcony with Zhou En Lai and others I did not recognize. In front of the Forbidden City there's a gigantic portrait of Mao.

                         Love, Jilly.

The college took the foreigners to Chengde, mountain resort of the emperors, with temples and garden scenery. The bus passed through drab villages. Harvest was late and traditional. Corn was cut with sickles, stooked by hand, carried to waiting mule carts, threshed and winnowed by hand. Riding in their glass coach the rich foreigners could imagine themselves back a century, seeing age-old processes – condensed, in their home countries, into a day's work for a combine harvester, driven by a solitary man wearing a breathing mask and ear muffs. The Chinese workers in pointed straw hats laughed and sang together.

Occasionally the visitors saw a tractor. Gloria, an excellent still photographer, wondered why she was interested only in taking pictures of mule carts and not tractors.

'Because you're looking for images that reinforce the stereotypes we bring with us,' said Francine. 'Such images seem more real than the reality before our eyes, ancient and modern mingled, and therefore contradictory. So we deceive ourselves and subjectively falsify our own perceptions.'

'How very French!' said Fox.

'They need more machinery,' said Irina, the Russian lady.

'That would bring unemployment,' said Francine.

'Various development projects have been tried,' said Ben, 'but there's a dead weight of inertia.'

'Administration in China is very poor,' said Ming. 'We lack trained managers.'

'Mao knew that,' said Ben. 'He saw that China had to move forward and get rid of the past. He started a moral and organisational crusade.'

Jilly was shocked.

'So temples and museums were smashed up, not to mention people's lives,' she said. How could Ben, wise and gentle, be so callous?

'The locomotives of history,' he said.

'What do you think of Mao, Ming?' asked Fox.

'He was a great revolutionary leader, but towards the end he made mistakes,' Ming answered carefully.

'Yes,' said Fox, 'the correct answer. I don't want the Party line. I'm interested in what you really think.'

Ming blushed. 'I am only interpreter. My opinion is not important,' she said, and refused, despite Fox's continued teasing, to say anything else.

Jilly had with her a copy of David Lodge's novel, *Small World*. Hoping the author would forgive her, she Xeroxed the first few pages. She explained Lodge's prologue as a witty analogue of Chaucer's: it set, she said, a pattern of expectation and was a comment on genre. Mentioning genre, she felt up to date.

Jilly read aloud Lodge's opening lines about April's sweet showers piercing the drought of March to the root, confidently and with pleasure, hearing inside her head the counterpoint of *The Canterbury Tales* .

Mei Ling said, 'Is Lodge social realist or is he a stream of consciousness?'

'Like most post-Joyce writers, he exemplifies both aspects,' said Jilly vaguely and coming to what she really wanted to say. 'Any English reader recognizes the allusions with enjoyment.'

Stony-faced sat her Chinese students. Jilly flipped. Any English reader? Exactly which reader or readers, Mrs Drybrook, are you telling the Orientals about? Do you really imagine, she asked herself, that a majority of English hearts palpitate to the rhythms of 'Oh, to be in England now that April's there', 'April is the cruellest month' or 'April, April, laugh thy girlish laughter'? Tags once assumed to be common property had become an expensive luxury. How many inheritors of the well of English undefiled could recognize, let alone pronounce, the opening lines of *The Canterbury Tales*? What did they know of

Chaucer on the Clapham omnibus or in the football crowd? How many English people, Jilly wondered as she stood in a run-down Beijing classroom, had even heard of him? Her own daughter's teachers at Henry Higgins Comprehensive had implied that Shakespeare was a racist imperialist reactionary, that literature was an instrument of domination by dead white bourgeois males, and there was nobody so wicked, naturally, as the white bourgeoisie.presumably her audience shared this opinion, which to her was barbarous. Her instinct was to laugh with *Private Eye* at Dave Spart, but she could hardly share the joke with the Chinese. What was she doing, offering spoonfuls from the great estuary of classical and Christian culture to these communist atheists? She must look for common ground. Today's pilgrimages, as Lodge pointed out in the book, she told them, were to meetings and conferences.

'Chinese only allowed to travel if they have permit from work unit,' said Fu Bing.

Wang Li yawned. 'We don't want literature,' he said.

'But that's what your government have hired me to teach you.'

Hubbub: 'No literature!' 'We want business English...' 'Make money!' 'We are sick of Dickens! We want modern book!'

'What modern book?' There was nothing available more recent than Hart Crane. American feature videos were piled, people said, in the customs shed, waiting for the censors. Anything that did get through was illegally copied by technicians in the viewing room and the list of holdings was a secret. Teachers smuggling in their own copies of classic movies were greeted with cries of: 'We've seen it three times already!'

Mei Ling said he wanted to study modern Western culture. Asked what he had in mind, he said he wanted to read interviews with Michael Jackson.

A deputation, polite but menacing, visited Jilly's flat. They cheerfully confessed to being lazy and said they had no intention of changing. The Party cadres could make life uncomfortable for Jilly, they said.

'We are working to get Mrs Alice deported,' said Fu Bing, the monitor.

'Why?'

'She is religious. Like you, she works too hard.'

'Oh, do we? Let me tell you, China will stay a Third World country until you develop Japanese work-habits, until people stop locking their offices and disappearing whenever they feel like it, until the secretaries stop being "too busy" to help us foreigners, but able to play Chinese checkers in the afternoon. You envy American wealth, but American prosperity is founded on hard work and self-motivation.'

The young people smiled.

'You are naïve,' said Fu Bing. 'Most foreign teachers start like you, enthusiastic. Soon we teach them Chinese way.'

'Get out,' said Jilly.

A little later Xiao Xu arrived on her own. Delicate blossom, she walked mincingly, a fastidious Oriental princess, glossy hair sleeked back from rounded ivory forehead. Skin colour among the students ranged from pink and white to swarthy, and they looked very different one from another. Xiao Xu was a beauty she and knew it. Sweetly she smiled, explaining that though she herself was a workaholic and thought Jilly a wonderful teacher, 'the others' wanted a teacher who would chatter innocuously throughout the two-hour teaching period.

'I daresay, so you can get on with reading Chinese newspapers at the back of the class. Sorry, but your government paid a lot of money to get me here and I'd be ashamed not to earn my salary. You all say you want "more discussion" in class, but often I ask questions and nobody says a dicky-bird.'

'What is dicky-bird?'

'It means a word. English slang.'

'Which word?'

'The word "word".'

'?'

'Never mind. I wish you would talk more in class.'

'You do not understand,' said Xiao Xu patiently. 'We say nothing because Party members spy on us and tell everything we say. In China, we must be careful. We trust nobody.'

And I bet Fu Bing sent you to soften me up, thought Jilly. A variant on bad cop, good cop.

'My parents are Party members. We are also secret Christians. You must tell nobody.'

'I won't tell anybody anything,' said Jilly, 'but why do you tell me? Why do you take such a risk?'

'I tell you so we share a secret and become friends,' said Xiao Xu, surprised at Jilly's innocence. 'I trust you. I tell what the others say behind your back, isn't it?'

'Perhaps you'd better not,' said Jilly firmly. She needed no counterspy and did not intend to be manipulated.

'When can I visit you?' persisted Xiao Xu.

Jilly named her office hours. Xiao Xu looked disappointed,

'I want you for my friend, not just my teacher,' she said, 'My foreign friend.'

Jilly thought the relationship should remain professional, but was at a loss how to say so. 'Foreign friends' was the euphemism for all visitors, and Xiao Xu might not realize she was being presumptuous.

Xiao Xu added, 'If the others visit you too often, they will be criticized.'

'Who's to know?'

'We must sign at the guard-house when we visit teachers, of course. I do not like Wednesday political meeting. Criticism happens then.'

'So why go?' Jilly had been a member of the Labour club at Durham.

'It is compulsory.'

'Oh.'

'They do not criticize me,' boasted Xiao Xu. 'I have *guanxi*, influence. My parents are important professors. In the Cultural Revolution, we suffered, but now is all right. My father's house had eight rooms. The government took all except one. Peasant families moved in. My mother is mathematician. She complained when schools were closed and was sent to countryside. Now she is rehabilitated. I was born in countryside. She could not take care of me. I was sent to my aunt, her fourth sister. Aunt was very cruel. I must wash all family clothes with my little hands. I must not eat with family, but after. Now I am not strong. I must go to hospital every two weeks for mineral injection. Do not tell my classmates.'

Jilly was uncertain whether the girl wanted pity as a victim or respect for her status. She suspected Xiao Xu of being sent to trap her into discussing religion or politics. Jilly consulted Ben as to whether Xiao Xu's story was likely to be true. The girl's own aunt, behaving like a wicked stepmother?

'Perfectly likely. She was the child of class enemies and the aunt could not afford to be seen showing kindness to her. Everybody here, including us, has a dossier, and a black mark is serious. Lots of couples were pressured into divorce because one of them had slipped up. People keep their heads down. Because it was traditional to drown girl babies, men in the countryside can't get wives. In the sixties and seventies, daughters of so-called "stinking intellectuals" were forcibly married to peasant farmers and told it was a privilege. Many of your students were born to couples like that. The women got divorced when things changed and hot-footed it back to the cities. Broken lives all around you, Jilly. One treads on eggshells here. Any sad story is likely to be true.'

Professor Chong warned Jilly that it was a mistake for her to let students know their marks except in end of semester exams. Students were complaining that her marking was too severe. Jilly assumed that

35 per cent was a bare pass and anything over 70 per cent denoted brilliance. Students were used to a system where 60 per cent was a bare pass and everybody expected marks between 70 per cent and 90. So Jilly marked more generously. He also told her to keep all student work after correction, in case the students should complain they had been taught nothing. Jilly wondered whether to confess about the threats, but decided against it. The prospect of 're-education' was unappealing.

On 'Teachers' Day' Jilly received greetings cards saying the students loved their 'respectable teacher, Mrs Jilly'. These were furtively handed, with whispers: 'Is a secret. Do not tell the others.' Jilly was beginning to feel that the country specialised in the manufacture of petty secrets.

The foreigners liked escaping to the Summer Palace, a short bike-ride away. However crowded that beautiful park became, it always seemed spacious and refreshing, as the long cloister ran along the lake. They photographed each other in front of the marble boat built by the last Dowager Empress Cuxi with money which should have been spent on the navy.

Ozymandias, thought Jilly. It struck her as like the Brighton Pavilion, a memorial to princely megalomania the world would have been poorer without. Which was more important, the misery of the labourers who built palaces and pyramids, or that the buildings should survive? Was such crazed magnificence of value? She asked Ben.

'The Chinese use artefacts like this for what they call "class education",' said Ben.

'The question of their aesthetic value remains unaddressed,' said Jilly.

'It is answered implicitly,' said Francine, 'by encouraging the people to enjoy them.' Francine was thirtyish, poised and elegant, although she always wore jeans. Fox was said to be paying court to her.

Jilly reflected that in capitalist Britain entry to museums and treatment in hospital were free, while in Communist China they had to be paid for.

A picnic party went to a reservoir in the mountains. Jilly found herself among the Russians and their students and they shared their food, sitting on the grass on newspapers. A young Chinese in a Mao suit took a fancy to Jilly and though they had no language in common took care of her, holding her elbow on the steep slope down to the boat. Jilly was flooded with joy: here she was holding hands with a Russian-speaking Chinese in a remote and beautiful landscape, as far away from the humdrum as could be imagined. She couldn't wait to tell Rosalind.

On the way back, Jilly sat with Irina, who was seconded from Moscow University and who was in her third year in China. Her job was waiting for her; she was lucky, she said. Many young people had no job. She was thrilled about Gorbachev's *glasnost* and *perestroika*.'We have waited fifty years for this!' she said, excited. 'It is not just reform, it is revolution!'

She found Beijing restful, she said, after frenetic Moscow, but China, so cheap to Jilly, was horribly expensive to her: buses and trains cost twice as much as in Moscow, food four times.

'Chinese students are not good linguists,' said Irina. 'They are anxious to reach ideas, so do not work at elementary details.' She added that from 1960 to 1980 nobody had studied Russian, so background was missing. 'Often the schoolteacher is bad and the desks are of mud, in the open air. But they have such terrible difficulties, one must respect even the weakest.'

In November it rained. Jilly had a stomach upset, she felt fluey, and the ten-minute walk across campus to the canteen soaked her feet. She asked Ming the Chinese word for wellies.

'You don't need!' cried Ming. 'Never rain in Beijing.'

Jilly looked out at the downpour.

'It's raining now.'

'Dry tomorrow,' said Ming. 'Do not waste your money.' Eventually she was persuaded to write the word in Chinese on a scrap of paper. In this way, Jilly coped with such things as dry cleaning. Jilly bought her wellies but Ming was right. Jilly wore them only once. The dust gave her a sore throat. Ming took her to the campus clinic, which had a couch with leg-clamps, Jilly assumed for abortions. The woman in a white coat scolded Jilly for not wearing more clothes. The weather was mild and Jilly wore only wool trousers and sweatshirt over minimal underwear. The doctor demonstrated severely her own three woollen sweaters and two pairs of long johns under her trousers, giving her the overstuffed look characteristic of mature Chinese women, and prescribed a throat spray of powdered melon rind, plus a course of penicillin injections. Jilly endured the first and was given a book of tickets and instructed to return every day.

'Is penicillin really necessary? I mean, is the infection serious?'

With some difficulty, Jilly grasped that penicillin was the standard treatment for colds. Jilly did not go back, but was tracked down by the doctor waving a syringe, saying she would be criticized if Jilly was not made better. Jilly submitted to daily punctures in her rear from a syringe which had been boiled and reused. Ming told her it was all right: there was no AIDS in China, and no homosexuals either.

Dear Rosalind,   November 6, 1988

Life here is unexpected. A fashion show on campus! Models were our students and a young electrician, one of our maintenance workers. Teachers' salaries are depressed because for every teacher there have to be two administrative staff and four manual workers, all of whom seem under-employed to me, all within the same budget. The models were all glamorous, expert disco dancers, in glitzy clothes, not flashy, really smart. The students went wild, except for a girl called Xiao Xu, who was snooty about the only girl in the group who rivals her for looks. Xiao Xu snorted, 'She looks like a lady of the street. She is only a peasant.' My colleague Alice, who is rather puritanical, walked out, because short skirts were 'immodest', an aspect of Western corruption. Professor Zhang once said women over thirty were criticized if they wore anything except black, blue or grey, but young girls here love bright colours, frills, denim and high heels. Only old men wear Mao suits...

Dear Pam,   November 6, 1988

I have had a few trips into the countryside. The villages are clusters of huts, stone, brick and mud, with small yards for pigs and fowls, no flowers, no vegetables except on communal plots, just dry mud. No frozen veg here. In the villages, they do their washing on stones in the rivers, in stagnant ponds and on the steps of canals, among the gently bobbing Coke cans, orange peel and polystyrene waste. They beat the washing with sticks, wring it out by hand, and hang it on lines stretched between trees. You see a lot of bedding hanging up to dry that's nothing much but patches hand-sewn on patches. Sewing machines are luxury items...

Pam's reply was indignant. Jilly only saw what she wanted to see and surely there was a network of communal launderettes? She envied Jilly her motivated students. Jilly put her letter aside.

Meanwhile, her students grumbled. They wanted modern literature. They told her she must search the pirate bookshops, forbidden to foreigners.

'If I mustn't go there, how do I manage that?'

'You must send a Chinese teacher, of course,'

With apologies, Jilly asked Ming to help. Ming went cheerfully and brought back a list of books in English, the most recent published in 1938. The class asked why she did not order books from England. That books in England were expensive surprised them. They demanded that she import a book, type and duplicate it. They needed a study book and it was her job to provide one. Jilly tried Professor Zhang, busy and remote, a woman of authority, not the timid foreigner Jilly had befriended in England.

'A whole book is difficult,' said Zhang. 'There are books of extracts. Librarian will help you.'

The librarian was a smiling man in a Mao suit, who could read a little English but barely speak it. He fished out a dismal collection of improving tales, each with a socialist message. Jilly was told it was the custom to assign a course book. The students groaned at it and so did Jilly. A few of the students owned the book already. Others reported it was out of print. Jilly suggested they might study it on their own but they insisted it was her duty to teach them. Chong advised Jilly to use the cyclostyled materials in the teachers' office. Yellow with age, brittle and coated with granular black dust, lurking in a corner were half-sets of stories by nineteenth-century Americans. Jilly gave her students a course of British fairy-tales, read aloud with animation, which kept them happy. Their favourite was Bluebeard.

6

Professor Zhang invited Jilly and Chong to dinner. Zhang and her widowed mother lived in a two-roomed flat up six flights of concrete stairs, bicycles and tired cabbages on every landing.

'Irina and Tanya tell me your Russian is excellent,' said Jilly.

'My education was disrupted, as I told you, because we started with English, then we had to learn Russian. My poor father was forced to learn Japanese after Manchuria was invaded. When my sister became a Red Guard, it broke his heart. She told him, "You are not my father", because he spoke to us in English. It was forbidden. Now everybody is encouraged to learn English. We have our jobs back now. Too late for my dear Baba.'

'Your sister was a Red Guard?'

'What could she do? Others criticized her for not being enough destructive.'

'What happened to her?'

'She killed herself,' said Zhang simply.

'Now we must all help each other, build the new China,' said Chong. 'I have a friend, political scientist, who went to Paris to study. No job when he came back, so I recommend him as English teacher.'

'Is his English good?'

'Very bad.'

'Then surely he ought not to be teaching English?'

'He needs the money,' said Chong coolly. 'He can always stay a page in front.'

'Couldn't he teach French?'

'Few people learn French. It is only a school, not a university, so it is not important.'

Jilly thought it was, but lacked the courage to say so. Social cataclysms presumably dictated alternative values.

At seven-thirty Zhang said, 'It is time for you to go now. I will see you home.' Pushing her bicycle, she walked Jilly all the way back to her compound, honoured guest.

'Thank you so much for the little dish with the picture of Big Ben,' said Zhang. 'But you must not give Chinese many presents; we cannot always reciprocate.'

Jilly fell in love with Chinese music and her students, now friendlier, lent her tapes, invited her to performances. She discovered that one of her pleasanter students, Zhong Hua, was a noted player of the Chinese harp. He was delighted when she went to hear him. She also visited, on his recommendation, the Palace of Minorities, where traditional song and dance were kept alive. During her lonely evenings she tried to hear the BBC, but found herself listening to Radio Moscow, Radio Japan and the Voice of America.

She spent her afternoons in the foreign teachers' office, correcting work. It was comfortable in that every teacher had his or her substantial desk and chair. There was even a sofa, an enamel bowl on a stand with soap provided, and a full thermos. In a corner were a teapot, a broken thermos, an empty tea tin, a half-full packet of detergent powder, several empty Nescafé jars, a foot of iron piping, empty cardboard boxes and an inverted ricebowl, all thick with dust. A wire mesh wastebasket leaked torn scraps of paper on to the floor. A twig broom stood idle. Jilly wondered why these people were incapable of throwing out rubbish: balconies in Beijing flats were cluttered with broken pots, baskets and enamel bowls. Sometimes a cleaner would poke her head round the office door with a cheery '*Ni hao*,' flick a duster over the desktops and disappear, closing the door with ostentatious gentleness.

The office was where Chinese teachers could find and consult the foreigners. Tai Pang, an elderly Chinese teacher of English, haunted the place. Desperate for the promotion she had missed, she sought reassurance over multiple-choice questions. She pestered all the native speakers in turn, so that they avoided her. She was convinced that a 'parking-free zone' meant the same as 'free parking', that 'molten lava and rocks shooting up everywhere' should read 'molten lava and upshooting rocks' because 'according to American grammar, adjectives should be parallel' and insisted it was so, tears in her eyes.

She told Jilly she wanted to go abroad so she could have a colour TV and washing machine. Tai Pang asked Jilly what luxuries she would take home from China.

'Will you be entitled to a fridge?'

'I've got a fridge.'

'Washing machine?'

'Don't need one.' Jilly explained she lived near a launderette. Tai Pang thought such an amenity must be wonderful. After mutual incomprehension, Jilly grasped that Chinese people returning from abroad had the privilege of spending foreign currency on scarce consumer goods. Tai Pang assumed that Jilly needed permission to buy a freezer or microwave. Tai Pang found it hard to believe that most people in Britain had them already without having to travel abroad first.

'You Western people so rich, so lucky!'

Tai Pang was always pressing on Jilly gifts of food. Jilly felt obliged to invite her to the flat for a meal. Tai Pang insisted on taking over washing up.

'Leave that!' scolded Jilly.

'Chinese women always help in kitchen,' reproached Tai Pang, patting Jilly's hand. 'You are my sister.'

Zhang, Jilly's next guest, confided that Tai Pang had in fact been abroad but had come home in disgrace after shoplifting a pair of socks from Marks & Spencer, so her luxury permits had been withheld.

'Poor woman, she is very bitter,' said Zhang, 'Before the Revolution against Culture, her family had land. She did not suffer as I suffered; I nearly froze to death in mud hut. She suffered in the head and was in mental hospital. Her husband was important member of the Party and she was class enemy, so he divorced her. She keeps asking to be promoted, but of course it is not possible. She has trouble in head still; she is emotional. She refuses her timetable. Soon she retires.'

Seemingly people were not easily sacked in China. Zhang told how a young married teacher had fallen in love with a girl student whose marks were poor. He had begged Zhang to pad them but Zhang refused. The girl left the college to live with him and he went on extended sick leave, was never in his home when visited and was thought to be moonlighting for a foreign company. Only two years' absence forced the university to sack him. The sack meant that his deserted wife would lose her home, for accommodation was tied to jobs. The man and his new girl were living in a flat provided by his new employer.

Zhang lamented the death of idealism, of public spirit. That evening they watched the TV in amazement as a lipsticked and mink-coated speakerine told viewers in padded clothes and cotton shoes that to get rich was glorious. Spending on fashion and scarce consumer goods was the key to combining the benefits of capitalism with the moral high ground of Marxist-Leninism to produce a new socialism 'with Chinese characteristics'. Beauty parlours were the latest thing. Jilly hadn't seen any, but just off campus was a scruffy hole in the wall labelled '*Guerlain salon de beauté*' with a sunbleached poster of Boy George in the window.

Everybody knew baldness could be cured by rubbing the right stuff into the scalp. The Friendship Store offered several brands together with packets labelled 'Erect' and 'Herculean potency'. Ben wondered aloud what would happen if he were to rub one of these into his bald pate. He set up a performing arts club, run by its own committee. Oral skills in English developed rapidly. His students, all teachers, lectured in English to the foreigners on Chinese art, Chinese philosophy, Chinese music. They adored him.

Jilly had never before belonged to a minority. People invited her to their homes and offered her tuition in Chinese in exchange for coaching in English. 'You are becoming Chinese,' people said kindly, intending a compliment. But she was not Chinese and felt her identity in danger of being swamped. Ben had lent her a book on culture shock. It said there were three phases: one, when everything seemed quaint and charming; two, when newcomers huddled together to grumble; and three, when they either went native or turned hostile to their hosts. Ideally, said the book, one should reach a 'mature acceptance', neither romanticizing nor vilifying. Jilly's feelings oscillated between affection and exasperation. Gloria's grumbling embarrassed her, though when Jilly watched the canteen cook dropping fag ash into the rice she was tempted to complain herself. She felt guilty about having better living conditions than Zhang. She became used to the niggling inconveniences of Beijing, but was pleased when she found living was cheap. She had a habit of economizing and bought frying tomatoes instead of salad ones. The stallholder pointed out in English that the price difference reflected a difference in quality.

'Where did you learn English?' she asked.

'I talk to foreigners,' he said. 'Anything else?'

'Just one carrot.'

Ceremoniously he presented her with a carrot and refused to take payment. He had the manner and the speech of an educated man. He was probably, thought Jilly, one of the dispossessed, a 'stinking intellectual' who had fallen foul of the system. Now he sold vegetables.

Jilly borrowed a video of *Brideshead Revisited* and the class studied that, with extracts from a copy of the book. They fell in love with it, humming along with the music. They asked, 'If Cara is Lord Marchmain's concubine, why is Sebastian polite to her?', 'Are Charles and Sebastian homosexual?', 'Are we supposed to like Sebastian?' They assumed the story was a satire on 'the religion of Catholic', an absurd barrier to the happiness of Charles and Julia. 'Why does Charles not become Catholic so he can marry Julia?' The idea of indissoluble marriage was incomprehensible to them, but they disapproved totally of the remarriage of widows, an insult to the memory of their husbands. Fu Bing said he disapproved of divorce. It was dangerous for the stability of society. Forgetting their inhibitions about class discussion, the girls argued that divorce meant freedom for women while the boys said it was a bad freedom.

They watched fascinated and in silence while Charles 'made free' of Julia's 'narrow loins', her scarlet nails digging into his back. Jilly was nervous about this scene and expected complaints, but none came. When a storm at sea threw the passengers on the liner violently about, the students roared with laughter. They laughed even louder at Lord Marchmain's deathbed, sure it was a satire on superstition. Jilly did not quibble with their interpretation, though her own was different. The story of star-crossed lovers moved them. With no secondary literature to pillage, they wrote what they felt. Mei Ling wrote of Waugh's Cordelia, 'She is wise and innocent and always judges sanely of the life around her.' Jilly felt vindicated.

Professor Chong complained. 'What a waste of time! You could have lectured on four British authors each week. Instead you watch television.'

Jilly argued for depth, pointing out that the class analyzed the dialogue and situations.

'No need for whole works,' said Professor Chong. 'Extracts are enough. They need informations.'

Jilly wondered what to do and went over Chong's head to Zhang. Zhang asked the students to evaluate Jilly's teaching and they were, to Jilly's amazement, enthusiastic. Jilly was told she could carry on.

Gloria, whose discipline was linguistics, pooh-poohed the idea of *Brideshead* meeting anybody's needs. It romanticized class privilege. Oxford and Cambridge should become postgraduate institutions.

'The students like the clothes,' said Jilly feebly. 'They love the voices.'

'Maybe, but the accent is yesterday's,' said Gloria, whose native Glaswegian had taken an Australian colouring.

'They loved the foxhunt,' said Jilly mischievously.

'They're a bloodthirsty lot, the Chinese,' said Gloria.

'They wanted to know if British people really lived like that.'

'What did you tell them?'

'I said that only a few ever did and perhaps a few somewhere still do,' said Jilly. 'I was brought up in the country, but I've never been on a horse in my life. But when I watch the old tally-ho, or Trooping the Colour, the Queen in her golden coach, I get a patriotic lump in the throat. I know it's only dimblebore warp and woof heritage industry guff, but – '

'Candyfloss for the masses,' said Gloria. With her shallow-cut features, she looked like a freckled frog. She cycled off to swim in one of the downtown hotel pools.

Mei Ling was a thin boy with a prominent Adam's apple and fine fuzzy down on his chin. He whispered to Jilly after class, 'Come with me tomorrow afternoon to hear Chinese folk music. It is special. Just for you.'

He walked her through dusty lanes until they came to a run-down concrete building, approached through the usual round gateway. He led her through corridors and into a classroom of children aged about twelve.

'Now,' he said smirking, 'here is a teacher from England, who tells about her country.'

Jilly was furious. But she knew Mei Ling was poor and sensitive about his shabby clothes. If she quarrelled with him in front of these children, he would lose face and possibly this part-time job he desperately needed. She asked the children to sing her a Chinese song.

They clearly didn't understand much English, so Mei Ling interpreted for her. They obliged with a standard pop song about *youyi*, friendship. Mei Ling took questions in Chinese, translating them together with Jilly's replies.

On the way back, Mei Ling grinned, pleased with himself.

'I'm very angry with you,' said Jilly. 'You tricked me. You made me lose face.'

'Foreigner has no face,' said Mei Ling blandly.

'In the West we do not respect liars. We think it important to tell the truth. You tricked me. I thought Chinese people were honest. If you had told me you wanted help to teach a class on Tuesday afternoons, I would have come prepared.'

'Please not be angry. You are my favourite teacher.'

'You wanted a mug to take your lesson for you.'

'Mug? It is like cup?'

'No, like stupid person. I'm not speaking to you at the moment.'

When she told her colleagues, Ben said, 'They seem frank and honest, but there's something Machiavellian about them.'

'At this moment I'm not feeling very pro-Chinese,' said Jilly.

'They are liars,' said Gloria. 'You have no friends among the Chinese. They bang on about how low their salaries are - '

'We wouldn't fancy living on one hundred yuan a month.'

'They don't,' said Gloria. 'Their families help them out.'

'Their families are just as poor,' said Ben. 'Take Li Wang, bright young teacher, Master of Arts, slated for promotion, who lives in the classroom on the fifth floor of the teaching block. He's doing four jobs to keep himself in Nike trainers and help his parents. His wife is expecting the one baby they're allowed, in the hope of being allotted a room with access to a kitchen and bathroom. Lots of young couples live with their parents. It's not unusual for three generations to live in one room.'

Jilly thought of Clytie, pregnant at fifteen, imagining she was thereby entitled to her own council flat and housing benefit. A dose of China would have done Clytie good.

Xiao Xu called at Jilly's flat to apologize for missing class. Jilly offered her another showing of the video.

'It is not necessary,' said Xiao Xu. 'I can talk to my classmates.'

'If you don't want to catch up on the video rerun, you'd better borrow the book.'

Xiao Xu disappeared with it and hardly showed up to class. She told Jilly she had been having private lessons in English since she was ten. Alice complained that Xiao Xu was hardly ever in her classes either.

'She says she has to go to hospital for treatment,' said Jilly.

'Then she should bring a note. She never does.'

'How do you find her written work?' asked Jilly.

'When she does any – and that's seldom – it's too good! I suspect she may be paying a foreigner to polish it for her.'

'Orally she's above average,' said Jilly.

'I don't like her attitude,' said Alice. 'She's a creep.'

'Perhaps we ought to dock marks?'

'I shouldn't if I were you. If students get bad marks, it has to be the teacher's fault. That's the theory. I already complained about her to Professor Chong and he just smiled. Mei Ling tells me Xiao Xu has *guangxi*, influence.' Xiao Xu now hardly ever turned up to class.

'Where is she?' Jilly asked the others.

'We don't know.'

Mei Ling stayed behind for a confidential word.

'Do not worry about her,' said Mei Ling. 'She sees video at home.'

'How does she manage that?'

'You show video here. Of course it is copied and she borrows the copy.'

'You know that's illegal?'

'It is very common in China. We have few materials. We are so poor, you are so rich. Respectable teacher, I have fallen in love with your mind. It is like a wave. And your beautiful voice, like BBC, like Thatcher.'

'That's no compliment,' laughed Jilly, gathering up her papers. She was dying for a cup of coffee.

'Do not laugh,' reproached Mei Ling. 'We love Thatcher. Strong woman. I surprise that the government allow Chinese to read *Nineteen Eighty-four*. It is what happens in my country.'

'You know I must not discuss politics or religion, Mei Ling. That book is about Russia, anyway. Do be careful what you say.'

'Now we say what we like. Now is the era of reform.'

'People have been shot for careless talk. Now stop it.'

He walked with her along the dark corridor.

'All we Chinese have a little melancholy in heart. We patient, we suffer, we not complain. My brother is worker in factory. He knows nothing else. I am lucky. For next generation, thing will better. What car you drive in England?'

'I haven't got a car,' said Jilly cheerfully. 'I use the bus and ride a bicycle.'

'You kidding! You are laughing me. In West, no bicycle, only car. Only in China is bicycle.'

'Not true. We have plenty of bicycles in Britain.'

'How many million bicycle?'

'I've never counted.'

'To be rich avoids boredom.'

Jilly spoke of jetset junkies, of drowned corpses in Hollywood pools.

Mei Ling sighed. 'You know how Chinese live, how poor?'

'We have poverty at home, people who live in the street,' said Jilly.

'I have seen photograph,' insisted Mei Ling. 'Foreigner – foreign people – have beautiful house.'

Jilly tried to tell him about slums and beggars in London, but he knew better.

'I think you drive a Mercedes in London,' he said softly. 'All foreigner rich.'

There was a party for the teachers, everybody bringing a dish and a bottle, with dancing. Chinese men politely asked Jilly to dance and held her stiffly in the ballroom position, then released her and gave accomplished displays of disco dancing. Fox, who could perform well in both modes, was paying ostentatious court to Ming. Alice was sitting out, alone, and so was Ben. Jilly joined him, as he was nearer her age group than others. She told Ben, who listened quietly, soft plump hands folded in his lap, what Mei Ling had said.

'To that young man,' said Ben with his usual slight formality, 'you are a visiting princess from Mars with green hair. You carry with you not only the traditional prestige of the teacher, but the glamour of exoticism and wealth. Don't dazzle him and don't get involved. Keep a distance.'

Fox was talking about his time at Oxford, 'punting all day and punting all night', which intrigued Ming. 'What means punting?' she asked. Fox, whirling her expertly, promised to tell her when she was older.

A pair of married teachers sang a duet which made the Chinese laugh. Alice explained it was about an arranged marriage: when the bride lifted her veil, the groom found her so ugly he preferred to sleep in the sty with the pigs.

'Are we all single because we're in China, or in China because we're all single?' wondered Gloria, for the party had drifted into two main groups, Chinese and the foreigners, except that Fox was sitting with Ming. Her eyes were bright in her plump little face.

'That girl over there,' said Fox in a low voice, 'asked me earlier, "Are you looking for a wife?" and when I said not at present, she said, "When you are, do not forget me".'

'The students all know about her,' said Ming. 'She has bad reputation. She wants to marry a foreigner and go abroad. They call her "Miss Passport".'

'Have you ever been tempted to marry, Ben?' asked Jilly.

'Tempted, often,' replied Ben urbanely, 'but never to marriage.'

'I don't believe you're such an old woman as you pretend,' giggled Gloria. Her ginger hair, normally pony-tailed, was flowing loose.

'You have drunk too much wine, Gloria,' said Francine, taking her firmly by the elbow.

'Time for bye-byes, light of my life,' said Fox, kissing Ming's hand, flustering her. 'You that way, we this way.' He handed her over to one of her room-mates.

Next day Jilly was accosted by Alice. 'Did you take my fork after the party?'

'No,' said Jilly, 'I brought two and took them back.'

Alice grunted. A notice appeared on the board: 'Will the person who took my fork after the party please return it at once. It is my ONLY fork.'

Gloria howled. 'Great advert for her social life! In China all this time and she's only got *one* fork!'

'She keeps asking me if I'm sure I didn't take it by mistake,' said Jilly.

Three weeks later, it still hadn't turned up and Alice was still nagging.

'Why don't you buy another one, Alice?'

'I'm waiting for the thief to do the honourable thing.'

'So how are you managing?'

'With a very large spoon,' said Alice grimly. 'That's the last time I mingle with the herd.'

Alice was grey-haired. Jilly's mousy hair had been pepper and salt for years. She wondered whether to dye it and consulted Gloria.

'It'll have to be black, unless you go to one of the big hotels, and they'll charge an arm and a leg,' said Gloria.

So Jilly's hair was dyed black, with Ming's help.

'You look younger,' said her students. 'You look Chinese! You are becoming Chinese!'

Ming went out of her way shyly to approve. 'You should dress up! It is good for you to use make-up.'

'You don't use make-up.'

'It is different,' said Ming. 'You are a Westerner. Do you think Mr Fox marry a Chinese girl?'

Ming had poor teeth and complexion and wore spectacles. In a nation where the average standard of beauty was high, she rated brains ten, looks three. Ming was making an effort, with high heels and bright sweaters, but Jilly thought Ming's chances with Fox were slim. Anyway, Jilly fancied Fox herself, though he paid her minimal attention. She said she did not know.

Ming said to Jilly, 'In China both men and women are expected to be virgin when they marry. But now many are not! They have affair. Chinese men go abroad, sometimes have affair with many women.' She blushed. 'Is it true that in the West you have group sex?'

Jilly could not help laughing.

'Not that I know of.'

'But you have homosexuals, right?'

'Some, of course, like everywhere else.'

'There are no homosexuals in China.'

'Really?' was all Jilly felt like saying.

'I like your blouse,' said Ming. 'How much?' Knowing that this question, together with 'What do you earn?', 'How old are you?' and 'Where are you going?', far from being rude, was a polite conversational gambit, Jilly told her. Ming was horrified.

'They cheat you!' she cried. 'You must bargain with them. I come with you.' They went together to the silk market. The stallholder turned surly. 'He says he will charge you double and share with me,' said Ming, shocked. Two Chinese women, overhearing, shouted angrily at the trader, who shouted back. Jilly and Ming escaped. 'Chinese people honest people,' insisted Ming. But other traders refused to do business with the foreigner and her Chinese watchdog. They tried the Friendship Store, reserved for foreigners, and expensive. The Chinese shop assistants refused to serve Ming, who wanted a shirt for her brother.

'It is like the park in Shanghai, "No dog, no Chinese",' said Ming bitterly.

'Let's get something to eat,' said Jilly. They ordered hamburgers and waited for ten minutes. Eventually the waitress snapped, 'Hamburber finish.' They changed their order to noodles, only to be told, in the triumphant tone Chinese menials use when denying a foreigner, 'Noodle finish'. Finally they secured hot dogs, to Ming's delight. 'Always I want to know what is hot dog,' she said happily. 'Now I know. It is delicious.'

Ming helped the foreigners buy train tickets. Forms had to be queued for and filled in, presented after more queuing with identification. Often all tickets for the day you wanted had gone but you might get one for a few days later. No return tickets, as trains were crowded and unpredictable hordes could not be accommodated. Places had to be kept for Party officials. China has few roads and internal flights are often cancelled. Somehow Jilly slipped away one weekend to see the caves at Datong, with a rock Buddha forty feet high. From the train she glimpsed mean villages, thick with television aerials. In Datong they manufactured steam locomotives. It was hard to breathe: the air was grey and thick with coaldust and sulphur fumes, yet several million people lived and worked there. On the nearby grasslands, Mongolian herdsmen were being encouraged to abandon their nomad way of life so that their children could go to school instead of tending sheep. Jilly saw a playground full of children in sheepskin hats with earflaps, and men on bicycles slung with raw, bloody skins.

Soon Gloria and Jilly took turns to cook, as Jilly had tired of canteen food. Fox often joined them. He bought himself a camcorder and said his documentary on 'the real China' would make his fortune. Gloria, an accomplished still photographer, told him he had no sense of selection.

One evening Ming dropped in on Jilly's flat. Seeing Fox, she blushed.

'Can you help me with this exercise I have to teach tomorrow?' she said demurely.

'Why didn't you telephone to make an appointment?' said Gloria. 'You're interrupting our supper.'

'But it is seven o'clock!' said Ming, who dined at five-thirty.

'We eat later than you,' said Gloria with her mouth full. 'We have office hours when we can be consulted. Now we are off duty and do not like to be disturbed.'

'I was teaching when Mrs Jilly was in the office.'

Gloria shrugged. Ming turned and left before Jilly could stop her.

'Was that necessary?' said Jilly.

'It's our business to help their professional development, not to help them stay one page ahead in the textbook,' said Gloria, picking up her chicken leg.

'Is there a difference?' Gloria, Jilly's guest, had turned Ming out of Jilly's own flat. 'We are guests in their country.'

'They use us for their own ends, don't you worry,' said Gloria, wiping greasy fingers on her napkin. Fox said nothing.

When Jilly next saw Ming, she apologized for Gloria. Perhaps, thought Jilly, I should have got up and run after Ming at the time. She had been taken aback.

'I know foreigners like to be telephoned,' said Ming, pained, 'but I do not have telephone when office is closed. I needed help. I know foreigners very busy and must not be bother...'

'You can always disturb me. Gloria has an unfortunate manner, that's all,' said Jilly.

'Unfortunate! Chinese people unfortunate, foreigners fortunate – all rich!'

It occurred to Jilly that she should perhaps have quarrelled with Gloria, but her instinct had been, shamingly, that her first loyalty was to a fellow Caucasian. Jilly had soon grasped that only the foreigners could easily telephone each other. Gloria grumbled about inefficiency: Jilly was beginning to admire Chinese skill in accommodating to hardship and difficulty, lacking amenities foreigners took for granted.

7

At home Jilly had lived in fear of bombs, either from Moscow or from the IRA. Knowing the crime rate was low, she felt safe in China. But then the strap of Francine's bag was slashed, and her money stolen, together with her precious papers, expensive and cumbersome to replace. Paranoia rippled among the foreigners. Francine threatened to move to Hong Kong or Taiwan. Yet Jilly's students wrote about how much better things were than in the days when 'everybody walked in fear; now China smiles again'.

Zhang, invited to eat with Jilly, asked what Jilly thought of China.

'I wish people wouldn't spit. And people smoke too much.'

'Indeed men do smoke too much. But spitting is forbidden. There are notices everywhere.'

'Nobody obeys them. The streets are foul.'

'In England I was shocked to see the streets foul with dog droppings. I liked the freedom in England, though. But with all its shortcomings, China is my home. You know, Jilly, in England I was attracted to a man, an English man. He wanted to leave his wife and marry me, but I said we must keep it spiritual. Sex is less important for us. You Westerners are sex-oriented, we are food-oriented,' said Zhang, sitting gracefully, trim in her black trousers and tan sweater.

'Ah,' said Jilly, 'not so much an East–West divide as a North–South one.'

'Young people today believe in love. I did not love my husband. I grew to hate him. He was angry because our child was a daughter. And before my eyes he drowned her, new-born baby, in the urine bucket. It is illegal, of course, but in the countryside it is still the custom.'

Zhang's delivery was more staccato than usual and she gave the nervous giggle Jilly had learned to recognize as a signal of distress.

'Wasn't he prosecuted?'

'He bribed the cadre who reported it as a stillbirth.'

Jilly did not know what to say.

'My menses stopped. That happened to many in that time. I had no more children and he beat me for being barren. He is dead now.'

Jilly wondered whether she should get up and throw her arms round Zhang. Such suffering was unimaginable. No wonder Zhang had raved over Clytie's beauty.

'Today nobody is forced to marry. But it is sad for young people. Often they marry and have a child, but cannot live together, ever, if their work is in different cities. The grandmother raises the child. The parents can meet once a year. The government pays the fare.'

'I should hope so!'

'Chinese couples are used to separation. If one partner goes to study abroad, the other must stay behind. And when they are together again, often they are not happy. I think a husband is not like a lover.'

'No.'

'And of course in China we must care for our parents. I earn five hundred kwai a month, [Jilly earned three times as much] but I must give money to my mother and also my father's third sister. She has been ill and I could not visit. So I had to send her a hundred yuan.'

'What responsibility is she of yours?'

'Her children and her husband are all dead.'

'Hasn't she got a pension?'

'Only professionals have pensions in China. Is it true that Western people neglect their parents?'

Jilly, beneficiary of the Welfare State, told Zhang of its promise (still honoured then, in 1988) to take care of its citizens from cradle to grave; of meals on wheels, home helps and free hospital treatment. 'You've seen for yourself,' she said.

'We must pay for medicines and for hospital. And we have socialism! My friend Professor Zhu is one of China's leading scholars. He was in prison twenty years.'

'What for? What had he done?'

'He studied in Chicago and translated American classics into Chinese. He was accused of cultural pollution. Now he is old and ailing, heart trouble. His wife is deaf. They live with Zhu's sister. Her husband hanged himself in bad times. Zhu's son is meteorologist in America; his daughter is married to American businessman. The children say to Zhu and his wife, "Come and live in USA", but it is very difficult. Not everybody is allowed. What will happen when Zhu and the others cannot take care of themselves? One of the children must come to do it. Your daughter, will she take care of you?'

'I doubt it.'

'Professor Chong's daughter is a problem. She does not like to study, she does not like to work. She has rich Japanese boyfriend and thinks he will take care. So many young Chinese today embrace the American dream, aim high without the necessary effort. Mao wanted to get rid of "stinking intellectuals": we were class enemies. For five years, no education, all schools and universities closed. Sometimes I wonder where the next generation of scholars comes from.'

One of Jilly's difficulties was that some students had been selected on political, rather than academic, criteria. Some had had intensive coaching, others had received only a few lessons in English from incompetent teachers. Majoring in English, Jilly's students had so many compulsory courses (computers, stylistics, international trade, lexicology, and Japanese) that they were overwhelmed. One of the girls shyly asked Jilly to check out a job application for a bilingual secretary with an American company, which went: 'I am a junior of the People's Normal University College, Beijing. After I graduates, I want to be a

miss in business. I would be qualify with it. I speaks Chinese and English flutely, also speaks a little bit Japanese.
Yours sincere,

Ling Li.'

Jilly gently modified this letter. Ling Li was wounded. 'I think,' she said with dignity, 'Chinese teachers should mark our work, not foreigner. Chinese more understanding.'

Jilly mentioned to Xiao Xu that somebody in the class might hint to Ling Li that Chinese teachers let through too many mistakes.

'Do not worry about her,' said Xiao Xu haughtily. 'She is a peasant. Only thinks of clothes and jewellery.'

Mr Da rang late one afternoon when Jilly was planning some preparation to say he was in the Weiban's office and there would be a concert and a party that evening.

'Why couldn't you have told me before?'

'Foreigners fuss too much, ask too many questions,' said Mr Da.

'Suppose I don't come?'

'You must come.'

Jilly consulted Ben. 'We like to have plans cut and dried in advance,' said Ben. 'They knew about this visit weeks ago but didn't tell us in case it fell through. They move from contingency to contingency. They have a different mental set because they don't have refrigerators.'

'Refrigerators?'

'They have to shop every day; no space to lay in stocks, so they work from day to day. Forward planning, in our sense, isn't a priority. When we try to get our diaries organized, we get on their nerves, and they say "Leave organization to us". They strike us as obstructive, but they have no power to change things. If we complain then our intermediaries get it in the neck for not keeping us *waiguo ren* happy.'

He told Jilly that Western businessmen working in China had to expect stagnation and resist the temptation to believe that difficulties were caused by their own mistakes. Chinese negotiators made hard bargains, pleading poverty and playing on guilt.

'As you can see from this place, Chinese bureaucracy is not well co-ordinated horizontally. It's authoritarian. Cadres at the middle level won't release any info, because the art lies in avoiding responsibility. The successful cadre is the one who blurs decisions and blunts commands: that way nobody can criticize him. Decisions must always be referred upwards.'

'So that's why they can't make up their minds till the last minute? I've been given three deadlines for my end of term exam. They keep changing it,' said Jilly.

'I think we'll give offence if we don't go to this evening's thrash. Somebody's prestige is riding on it.'

In reply to a postcard from Lolo asking what the mysterious East was like, Jilly replied the city was a concrete jungle and the parks were without flowers because, according to Ming, they would be stolen.

'We had some exotica last week, a visit from Japanese performers. The Chinese will never forgive the Japanese for invading, but conceal their hatred because they want Japanese investment. The Nips want Chinese markets, so send their song and dance troupes to soften the Chinks up. Ming, our minder, said bitterly, "In 1950 the Japanese were as poor as us and now look at them!" The star was a plump chap in drag and horsehair wig, looking like something off a Christmas tree, wearing a dressing gown and white socks. His dance was an exercise in minimalism: hardly moved, merely posed. Very very slowly he lifted one arm and a gasp of suspense went through the auditorium. Then, still slow motion, he dragged a fan from his sleeve and – suddenly – flipped it open. Then he tripped once round the stage on twinkling fairy feet and that was it! After the interval he carried a load of plastic blossom across his shoulder like Dick Whittington's bundle, putting it down, fluttering hands, and picking it up again with neck jerks. A chorus of chaps in grey pleated skirts knelt down at the back of the stage yowling like cats. Perhaps I'm the Stone Age observer who can't see the point of Beethoven? There was a banquet afterwards with some of our students dressed up in Japanese costume with skewers in their hair. Professor Zhang whispered to me, "I think they are sheep in wolf's clothes"...'

Mei Ling continued to hang around Jilly. His face was girlish but his voice was deep. Like many Chinese men, he wore Cuban heels. His shoes were cracked.

'What do you think of nihilism?' he asked.

'What about it?'

'In Cultural Revolution, many kill themselves. I understand. Cultural Revolution over, still government interfere – interferes – too much.'

'Hush,' said Jilly. 'Walls have ears. Are you trying to get me into trouble? I will not discuss politics or religion.'

'But they have interest! Socialism not work. My brother has only work. Sunday he not know what to do. In England you have much rooms, car. Chinese spend money on food: if they want Walkman, they save in the mouth – less food. Now is reform, is OK – but too slow.'

'Do be careful what you say!'

But Mei Ling was having an orgy of subversion. Words tumbled out, grammar slipping under emotional pressure. 'Why we want Tibet?'

Minerals and atomic testing sites, I imagine, thought Jilly.

'Living space?' she suggested.

'Chinese not want to go there,' said Mei Ling. 'Government offer luxury hotel to teachers, but nobody goes except they forced.'

'Border defences? What about Pakistan?'

'Pakistan? We easy beat them! We have more people, most in the world!'

'*Tai ji*, eh?' said Jilly, using the Chinese expression that means 'too many people'.

'You learn Chinese? I teach you,' said Mei Ling.

'I'm too old,' said Jilly. 'Yes, there are too many people. Not enough space left for pandas or elephants – '

'Why do foreigners worry with animals? People important, not animals. Our problem to have enough food, good house.'

Jilly knew what he meant. Just off campus the tailor who made trousers ('So cheap!' said the foreigners) lived in a narrow cupboard with a bed at the back and the ever-whirring sewing machine on the table. The toddler was corralled in a teachest, a makeshift playpen.

Christmas was not celebrated in China, though secular greetings cards were exchanged. The foreigners could take two days off work, a special privilege. They combed the city's hotels for imported mince pies and chocolate logs, gloating over the loot. They went in taxis to a hotel where George Bush had recently stayed and ate a dinner which cost each of them a Chinese labourer's weekly wage, but 'worth it, this once!' Gloria produced a card from home which read, 'Here's one Aussie patriotic enough to send you a Christmas card – as against a BILLION CHINESE who couldn't care less.' They laughed till tears ran down their cheeks.

Gloria recited:

'Which I wish to remark
And my language is plain,
That for ways that are dark
And for tricks that are vain,
The heathen Chinee is peculiar,
Which the same I would rise to explain.'

'For heaven's sake, Gloria!' said Ben. 'The waiters understand English.'

'Only hotel English,' said Gloria.

'Some of them are graduates, and know enough to be offended. Shut up!'

He politely asked the waitress where she had learned to speak English so well.

'I graduate from People's Normal University College,' she said proudly.

'There you are! One of ours,' said Ben to Gloria, who for once was abashed. When the bill came she argued that as tipping was illegal in China the American-owned hotel had no right to add a 15 per cent service charge, but was persuaded finally to pay her share. Among the teachers of English, only Alice was absent. A sticker on her door, in Chinese characters, said 'Jesus saves'. It was rumoured that she celebrated Christmas, unlike the others, by going to church.

Everybody else rolled in at midnight. In the taxi were Ben, Gloria, Jilly, Francine and Fox. The car was stopped at the outer gate. 'He says nobody's allowed in after midnight for security reasons,' said Ben.

'But we live here!' protested Gloria. 'That means strangers, not us.'

The guard spoke again in Chinese to Ben, who said, 'We must get out and show our ID.' The night was cold.

'This is outrageous!' roared Gloria. 'You know perfectly well who we are: you see us every day! Don't you understand English, you slit-eyed yellow bastards?'

'Let's hope to heaven they don't! Do shut *up*, Gloria. Do you want to provoke an international incident? We'll just have to walk.'

They paid the taxi and, shivering and giggling, crossed campus to the inner compound where they had to wake the porter to unlock the gate and let them in.

Fox, generally quicker to accept invitations than to offer them, invited the others in for a nightcap. 'See a movie, turn on?'

'I've drunk enough already,' said Francine.

'I'm too upset and my feet are killing me,' said Gloria. Jilly and Ben drank tequila steadily in Fox's flat, but when Fox rolled a joint, Ben said goodnight, leaving Jilly alone with Fox. She did not admit she had never tasted tequila before nor smoked a joint. At last she was joining the grown-ups. 'See a movie?' said Fox. His flat was full of electronic goodies, including a video. He put on a tape of *Emanuelle,* but only bothered to watch it intermittently. Instead, he told her dreamily about carnival in Rio: 'Bizarre. Not just the costumes and the music and the drugs, fantastic, you can have sex with anybody you like, people running through the streets naked...at Oxford, there was very little sophistication...too many grammar school boys, making their first experiments with sex...that's what school's for...watch this bit, it's amazing...'

Jilly, a grammar school girl at Durham University, did not like to admit that her drink had been beer, her drug aspirin and her only sexual partner at college had been Robert, as inexperienced as herself. Soon she was giggling and telling Fox she loved him. Half her clothes were off and they were kissing. Her cheeks felt numb and fireworks were exploding inside her head. Soon his skilled fingers were making fireworks explode lower down. All their clothes were off. But nothing came of it. 'Sorry,' he said limply and fell asleep. Jilly threw up, just making it to the bathroom, dragged on her clothes and let herself out as quietly as possible, snapping the Yale lock behind her while Fox snored. Next morning her head throbbed and she was embarrassed to look at herself in the mirror, a haggard woman with dyed hair. I look like Dirk Bogarde in *Death in Venice*, she thought.

Fox woke in the small hours to find a Chinese thief in his room, sorting through his collection of videos, imported illegally via the diplomatic bag. Fox swore at him in Chinese and the burglar, rattled, snatched up a couple and ran, escaping through the French window. Jilly and Gloria had flats on the first floor and their French windows gave on to balconies. Fox's was on the ground floor. Snatching a robe, for he was naked, Fox dashed to the guardhouse to raise the alarm. The old man grumbled that he had been woken up not once but twice that night and foreigners were a bloody nuisance. He was still on his iron cot. He told Fox that Fox's Chinese was so bad nobody could understand it. Scratching his grey head and yawning, he said, 'What do you want me to do? Chase him?'

'Call the police, you old baboon!'

'At this time of night? No way. In the morning, maybe.'

Heaving himself up, he flourished his heavy bunch of keys and ostentatiously locked the main gate of the foreigners' compound. When Fox asked why it had not been locked, the old man muttered something about bothersome foreigners coming in late. Fox missed cash and an expensive wristwatch, but got little sympathy because the lock on his front door had been picked.

'It is your fault,' said Mr Da severely. 'You should bolt your door from inside.'

'Why wasn't the gate locked?' said Fox.

That question nobody could answer. Broken glass was cemented to the top of the high periphery wall. It was assumed the thief must be one of the builders living in temporary huts on campus, as nobody else could have got past the guards on the outer gate.

Gloria snorted that the system of guards was a sham, easily breached by what she suspected to be bribery. 'It keeps us out and lets them in. Some security! It's only so they can spy on us.' Fox, having lost his ID without which life was impossible, was with the Bureau of State Security downtown, filling in forms and paying for replacements.

'How was your little party?' Gloria asked Ben. 'Fox is a wanker. He does tell porkies.'

'Does he?' said Jilly, Venus pining for Adonis.

'We drank a lot of tequila,' said Ben, smiling at Jilly.

'He told Francine he had worked for Mossad, he told me he was a double agent for BOSS – ' said Gloria.

'Told me he worked for the CIA, but I don't believe him,' said Ben. 'He's a fantasist. It doesn't matter.'

'Alice thinks he's Antichrist because he told her he was a Communist.'

'Perhaps he teasinged her, as one of my students put it,' said Jilly.

'Odd, her living here, when she hates Marxism so much,' said Ben. 'I can reconcile it with religion.'

Gloria said, 'Then there's his story about a black lover who died of AIDS! I've never seen anybody so vain. He's pathetic, a drifter, a teacher of English to foreigners with big dreams. All that crap about living with guerrillas and selling pictures to newspapers!'

'He seems to have plenty of money,' said Jilly.

'I suspect he's an old-fashioned remittance man, black sheep; family pay him to stay away. Have you noticed his hair, dark at the roots?' said Gloria.

Ben said nothing, but later had a quiet word with Jilly.

'Please forgive me for interfering, but you're a very nice person. I'd hate to see you hurt. I didn't know the other night whether you wanted to be left alone with him or not. I wondered whether I should have protected your reputation. You were observed leaving late at night and Mr Da knows why the door wasn't bolted from inside. That young man tries to be all things to all men. He's a left-wing fascist, afraid of competition. He's like a cock in a farmyard full of hens. He could be dangerous.'

'Thank you for your concern, Ben, but I can take care of myself.'

'That's all right, then,'

Jilly wondered whether she ought to be tested for AIDS but did nothing about it. She wondered whether attraction to Fox was incestuous, sexual desire for the son she had never had. Fox seemed to be avoiding her and paid marked attention to Francine.

Gloria was enraged again by the sudden restriction on the pool in the hotel where she swam: on New Year's Day it was transformed into a private club for Japanese businessmen.

Radio Moscow announced that the Russian government was about to destroy all the chemical weapons it had previously denied having.

Cold and bright, sun shone on snow. The maintenance workers on campus made a snow panda, with coal-dust eyes, red felt tongue and wool scarf, a work of art. Children, usually subdued, lobbed snowballs, screaming happily, and their teachers joined in. Gloria spent less time with Jilly.

Dear Rosalind   4 January 1989

The other day a middle-aged Chinese man stopped me on the stairs and asked me how he could get to study in America. When I said I was British he asked me to sponsor him for a British university. Too many people are convinced that if they can pass a language test (one that demands a knowledge of baseball!) this entitles them to free tuition at a Western university. Lots of Americans here, Brits thinner on the ground. I keep getting Radio Moscow instead of BBC. The Russkies keep saying, in English, how they have more freedom and democracy now thanks to reform...

Ming, always humble and unassuming, asked if she could bring a friend to see Jilly. Ming was overworked and taken for granted, and Jilly liked to do her small favours. When Ming offered to cook for her Jilly gladly bought the food.

'She is nice girl,' said Ming, 'very clever. We make *jaozi*, Chinese dumpling, for you.'

Jilly took the hint and lashed out on good meat, extra-lean beef mince. The girls tut-tutted. 'Too dry,' Ming said and went out to buy pork fat. Ming's friend said nothing, but smiled and smiled.

Ming explained that her friend understood some English but spoke none. She was even plainer than Ming, in a shabby home-made jumper, shiny serge trousers and worn high-heeled shoes.

'She sleeps in her office because her brother has married and brings his wife home to their parents. My friend's mother criticizes her, says it is time she married and left home. She is ambitious: she wants to go to America and study computer.'

The girls were fascinated by Jilly's bras and pants hanging in the bathroom.

'You have same underwears like us!' breathed Ming.

Later Ming said to Jilly, 'My friend says you are not at all like a foreigner.'

'What did she think a foreigner would be like?'

'Rich and arrogant,' said Ming frankly. 'You are modest and common, like us. Do you think I could find a foreign man like you to marry?'

Curiosity was mutual. Fox said he couldn't take a slash without Chinese men peering.

'I wish they didn't *stare*,' said Gloria.

'Pale hair, big noses, we're asking for it,' said Jilly.

'One of our girls who works at the Embassy is going to marry a Chinese man!' said Gloria. 'She doesn't speak any Chinese and he doesn't speak English. Can you imagine anybody wanting to marry a Chinese man?'

'Possibly a Chinese woman?' suggested Jilly.

'They often find us repellent,' said Ben. 'Hairy, like monkeys. To them we stink. Literally.'

Ben's bald patch looked like a tonsure but the hair on his hands was thick. He was short and stocky.

'A gay friend told me Chinese men aren't normal in their development; can't grow beards till they're forty,' prattled Gloria.

'They fathered large families all the same till the government put a stop to it,' said Ben. 'Let's talk about something else.'

'Chinese men are like everybody else,' said Francine. 'I was married to one once.'

'What happened?'

'He left me.'

'I had a visit from "Miss Passport" the other night,' said Fox.

'I hope you didn't take advantage of her,' said Ben.

'She took advantage of *me*. It was rape. And then students came in a deputation and told me she was twenty-eight and not twenty-three, she was desperate etcetera.'

Ben looked disgusted.

'We should try not to behave like monkeys,' he said.

'What do you mean by that?'

'Monkeys are hospitable to friends and hostile to strangers,' said Ben.

'Oh, you're always preaching,' said Gloria.

8

Mr Da announced a bus trip to meet famous writers. This turned out to be an international press conference, with an admirable interpreter, who said that with 542 members the inner committee had become a little unwieldy, so an inner inner committee had been appointed, comprising the 109 writers present.

'There is a problem,' said the interpreter, a pretty girl. 'They are all elderly, but Mr Ping, who is eighty-eight, is still doing wonders, though alas too ill to be here this afternoon.'

Mr Ping was applauded in his absence and Mr Wong, who looked at least eighty-five, and waxy like a corpse, took the chair. An overcoat was wrapped round him like a shroud. American journalists asked questions about free speech. Mr Wong, via the interpreter, said there were two schools of thought. The idea that art was only a tool of politics was a Russian idea, not a Chinese one. On the other hand, *glasnost* and *perestroika* in the Soviet Union under Gorbachev seemed to be going further than the Chinese felt like following. All Chinese artists and writers were busy with reform. Pressed to describe this reform, Mr Wong closed the meeting. The hall was freezing cold.

Rosalind wrote to say she was pregnant and would be marrying when the legal side had been arranged. 'He's Reform. He may have to leave his congregation, but we shan't starve as he's trained in family counselling. My mama is pleased, as she was always afraid I'd marry out...' As an afterthought she added that Clytie and Charles were going through a rough patch. I daresay they are, thought Jilly, who sent dutiful postcards but received no reply. She pondered the various meanings of the word 'reform'.

Fox showed his students a video of *A Chorus Line* and Xeroxed the entire script to distribute. Mr Da sent a message to be careful with paper. Xiao Xu rarely came to class but visited Jilly at home, self-invited. Ming, she told Jilly, was a Party member, not to be trusted. Jilly wondered whether free speech was as safe as Mei Ling seemed to imagine. She did not trust Xiao Xu.

'We do not like Mrs Alice,' said Xiao Xu. 'She says we cheat.'

'And don't you?'

'It is Chinese way to work together. Mrs Alice says we must all work alone and not help each other. We know she understands Chinese, so we whisper in her class, "Old maid, old maid".'

'That's cruel,' said Jilly.

'She is foolish. Why do foreigners not marry?'

'I was married. My husband died.'

'Many people died in the Cultural Revolution.'

'Our revolution happened three hundred and fifty years ago. We cut the king's head off.' She knew that, according to Marx, Britain would be the last country to achieve the Communist Utopia. The Communist Utopia of China was all round her, as full of contradictions as the wicked capitalist West, which they despised yet envied.

'Now it is good again,' said Xiao Xu, 'to be intellectual.' Superciliously she tossed her glossy head, wiggled her slender hips and swayed out of the room, a flower in the wind.

The first semester ended later in January and the various universities arranged for the foreigners to travel at reduced rates. Jilly went down the East coast in a party, chaperoned by Ming. Each university had its Chinese representative. Local guides, self-taught, had impenetrable accents and were uneasy with questions. One said, 'The city is on a Plato. Resources of the river is in the fountains. The journey will cost you two hours. The martyrs were killed to death. Inside the temple seats a good-looking Buddhist...' not a man in a brown robe but three golden Buddhas, past, present and future, blue curls like grapes.

Another guide told them gambling was illegal in China.

'We know. And cards are played for money on the pavements of Beijing.'

'Do you report them?'

'Why should we?'

'Reward!'

'Not our business.'

'So rich you do not want reward? Report is public duty! Some are professional gambler. In Shanghai a clothworker sold cloth worth one thousand kwai to pay for his gambling; used all his money and his wife's as well. She left him. His daughter-in-law had no money for hospital when she give birth, so she divorce husband. Other two sons kill themselves because the family lose face. Their sister so angry she set fire to house and gambler go mad. So you see, gamble is very bad.'

'Very bad,' agreed the foreigners, spluttering with mirth. Jilly hoped the guide's feelings were not hurt. She visited the silk factories of Wuxi, the scenic gardens and lake of Hangzhou, watched shoals of fish netted like silver pennies, a miraculous draught, went to the Garden of the Humble Administrator, all pavilions, water, rocks and curving corridors, variety in a small space. Paintings were on sale and the foreigners bought.

'You pay too much,' scolded Ming. 'I hear him tell guide he does not paint picture himself; he buys them at one-tenth the price and shares profit with guide.' She was shocked.

Ben shared a room with Fox, the Russian ladies shared, so did Gloria and Francine, and Jilly was with Ming. Fox teased Ming that he should share his room with one of the women. Ming said he was a bad man and it was not allowed.

Jilly showered every day and modestly wore a dressing gown between bathroom and bed. Ming had no dressing gown and no nightdress and did not seem to take showers. She slept in her 'underwears'. Lying awake, she told Jilly about her family in Inner Mongolia and her brother at the Petroleum University in Beijing. Peasants and workers, her family had not suffered. They were steadily getting better off. She was the first generation in her family to go to unversity.

Neatly she made her own bed. Jilly gently told her it was unnecessary. The *fuyuyuan*, chambermaids, would see to it.

'Luxury!' cried Ming, awed. 'I never stay at hotel before.'

Guides and interpreters ate at a separate table. Ming, the only woman among them, didn't get enough to eat as the men grabbed so much. Jilly and Francine begged Ming to join them at the foreigners' tables, but she stuck to her place. 'It is forbidden,' she said wanly.

They travelled on trains 'soft seat', first class, another new experience for Ming. Fox teased her, asking her whether she thought he should marry a Chinese girl.

'That is not for me to say,' said Ming with dignity.

'I don't think I shall,' said Fox carelessly. 'I've been warned. You're soft and sweet till you catch us but as soon as you become pregnant you bob your hair and become scolds and tyrants. The husband has to hand over all his money and beg for cigarettes.'

Ming's lip trembled. 'That is true,' she said bravely. 'We say Chinese husband like sheep tied to bedpost. I hope to marry one day. Everybody needs a family.'

Patiently she smoothed the way, helping the foreigners with shopping and everyday problems. Gloria said Ming was sly, because she told Ben she liked Australian informality and disliked British coldness, but told Fox that she disliked Australian familiarity and admired British politeness. Francine said Ming was merely exemplifying the Chinese notion of good manners.

Jilly, hearing Ming sobbing gently in the night, pitied her.

They saw tea growing and went into various peasant homes, clean but bare. Floors were naked concrete, walls unpainted plaster. Some had an old brick *kang*, a bed heated by burning straw underneath, which seemed a good idea until Ming pointed out that the smoke dried throats and irritated eyes. People proudly displayed colour TV sets, the only gadgets visible.

Ming said 'When television first came a few years ago, everybody thought it was wonderful. The millennium had come. Now we know that is not true. There is more to life than television.' The foreigners were in themselves objects of curiosity, an entertainment, and the Chinese people eagerly compared ages with them.

Jilly went on a different trip to Harbin, in the north, nineteen hours by train from Beijing. The journey was uncomfortable, as there weren't enough 'soft seat' places and Jilly travelled second-class with Ming in an unheated carriage with no doors, so cigarette smoke drifted in from the corridor. Ice thickened on the inside of the window. Breath froze. Ming said it was much more comfortable than 'hard seat', third class, her usual way of travel. In the hotel a menu offered bears' paws and moose lips, but these delicacies were not to be had. Ice sculptures evinced a chaste translucent beauty: a crystal wonderland of pagodas, bridges, arches, stairs, with bears, lions, monkeys, swans, cranes, lotus flowers. The river was frozen a foot thick and people walked on the ice, skated, tobogganed, while others hired sailboats on wheels, powered by the icy wind, at minus 30 degrees. The air 'burned frore', thought Jilly, remembering her Milton: 'Chineses drive their canie wagons light.' A rectangular hole had been cut in the ice and young men were swimming, diving, thrashing about and scrambling out before diving in again. There were no warm towels to comfort them. They padded on naked feet, in skimpy bathing slips, across the solid ice, swept by bitter winds. Jilly took off one of her thick gloves and dipped her bare hand in the water. Now I know what frostbite feels like, she thought. Awed, she watched the swimmers going in and out of the water. She knew Harbin had recently had a drug bust.

'Are they criminals? Is this a punishment for them?' she asked Ming.

Ming laughed. 'It is for fun! Winter swimming is good for colds and rheumatism. Old people do it.'

Returned from holiday for the second semester, Jilly found a letter from Rosalind. Clytie and Charles were having a trial separation and Clytie was staying with Rosalind, who she believed had always understood her. Rosalind was not sure whether the breach was permanent or whether Clytie just 'needed space'. 'Apparently,' wrote Rosalind, 'every time they have the slightest argument, he screams she doesn't love him and pops half a bottle of aspirins or pulls a polythene bag over his head or slashes his wrists. I gather he's been known to hit her.' Oh God, thought Jilly. That's all poor Clytie needs. Whatever possessed me to call her Clytemnestra? Greek tragedy; bathtowels splashed with blood, slowly reddening water. Clytie was excited about Rosalind's coming baby and was fussing over Rosalind, promising to look after the child when it arrived, or at any rate to do some babysitting. She needs someone or something to love, thought Jilly with a pang of guilt. Charles must be a shit. At Clytie's wedding, his distinguished parents, both remarried, had stood together for the photographs, then avoided each other throughout the reception.

A stranger knocked one afternoon on Jilly's door and introduced herself as Hannah Wong. She was pretty, a natural blonde, and her teeth were a credit to the orthodontics industry. She had a soft American accent and wore pastel college-girl clothes.

'Bruce, that's my husband, teaches English at the business university, but he's really writing a project on Chinese socialisation patterns,' she chattered. 'We're newcomers to campus. We lived at the

Friendship but now they're refurbishing and they found space for us here. Bruce's family are ethnic Chinese, but he's third-generation American and my, doesn't that give rise to some confusions here. I've come round because I ought to get acquainted with the group and there's nothing to do here evenings except watch Chinese TV and I can't get to watch ours because Bruce's computer interferes. He plays chess with it. All the time. I'm not sure it was the right thing, coming here. I just hated New York, the rat-race, you know? So competitive, so selfish. I hoped China would be different, a more natural way of life, but we've been here year and a half and I'm not so sure. And there are problems with Reuben, that's my kid, looks kind of Chinese with a different father and all, but his skin and hair are lighter, he gets bothered all the time, people touching him. Goes to a Chinese school and I see him able to read Chinese comics and I think, well, it's an ethnic and cultural heritage, we've been able to give him something American kids don't generally have, his father doesn't speak any Mandarin, but the gender conditioning here is totally rigid, Reuben's acculturated into passivity, you know, like shut up, don't ask questions, no child-centred activity methodologies in China, the resistance Bruce gets you wouldn't believe. Bugs me that Chinese kids sit on buses, adults stand up! I tell him he should stand for grown people but if he does they laugh and refuse and he gets cranky.When he stands he's on a level with all these Chinese butts and he, like: "Aw mommy, there's another one let off a fart", and I'm so mortified I pray to God there's none of them understands English. I'm bored to socksville here. I pick up the apartment mornings, but it doesn't last all day. I know Beijing: I can tell you where you can buy bread, real mayonnaise, decaffeinated coffee, cheese, Chlorox, pot scourers; the market stall near Janguomenwai has the best dry noodle, Wangfujing's no good for food; the only safe place to buy honey's Woudako, the regular honey'll poison you. Give me a good old American hamburger, I know what I'm eating. Candies are no problem here, Reuben doesn't have any cavities,

Bruce says candies are a bad habit but I *need* sugar. I was into feminism a while back but it doesn't seem to be the answer, does it? Bruce was my professor and he seemed so *sophisticated*, you know. Now he doesn't pay enough attention to my needs.'

'Perhaps you're rather demanding?' Who was this woman and why should Jilly be interested?

'I'm his *wife*. He'd rather be married to his goddamn computer!'

Jilly did not find it easy to get rid of her. Soon she was back, complaining that the foreign community were not friendly. She found Gloria 'hostel'. Jilly admitted that Gloria was a little prickly. Gloria treated Hannah as a joke and cruelly mimicked her.

Mei Ling's straight hair had been tortured into a curly perm. He said to Jilly, 'China will never modernize while she is run by mediocre. If you are not good student, you join Party, get good job. Clever people don't get good job. The Party fear them.'

'It isn't easy to join the Party, is it?'

'Very hard,' said Mei Ling. 'I try, they don't have me. I wanted to do postgraduate, but I did not do well in politics.'

'Don't get into trouble,' said Jilly. 'And be careful what you say.'

'This is the time of four modernisations. I translate Western literature into Chinese, Jeffrey Archer, Danielle Steele,' said Mei Ling.

'You have to pay,' said Jilly.

Mei Ling was indignant. China was poor, he was poor: could never afford it.

Jilly tried, without success, to explain copyright and intellectual property.

China needed books, argued Mei Ling. 'I want to translate Western medical book, bring sex education to China. We are very poor in sex. Do you have this book with you?'

The students were in their final year and for the first time had to find their own jobs. Last year's students had been slotted into posts by the authorities. Xiao Xu wanted to get a job with an airline, but jobs were reserved for relatives. Even for those with the right connexions, the answer was often, 'We don't hire girls.'

'Isn't equality of the sexes built into the law?' Jilly asked Xiao Xu.

'Of course,' said Xiao Xu. 'But the business people do not like intellectuals. And they don't hire girls. Will you support my application to American university?'

Alice told Jilly with some irritation, 'She doesn't have to worry about her grades to get on postgraduate courses in America. She will have good references from Chinese professors: one is Professor Chong, the other her mother.'

'Won't it look suspicious, having the same name?'

'The surnames are different: the mother keeps her maiden name, like all married women in China.'

Xiao Xu explained to Jilly, 'When I come back with my Master's or doctorate, I shall be too old to marry. Anyway, nobody will marry me because I was born in unlucky year.'

The country girls who cleaned the foreigners' flats and changed their sheets worked long hours for small reward. They lived in their own building and were solaced by visits from the building and maintenance workers, many living without their wives. Pam wrote to Jilly asking about the People's Paradise. Jilly was too busy to answer.

Tai Pang returned, worried about this sentence: 'Paris has a heart; Vienna whirls her admirers away on a cultural waltz; New York has no soul.' 'What does it *mean* ?' she asked plaintively.

'Not much,' said Jilly. 'The writer likes Paris and Vienna but doesn't like New York.'

'Cultural waltz? What is that?'

'I don't know,' said Jilly, who was correcting written work.

'"When he played the Kreutzer Sonata, the fire and stars were in it"! What is doing the fire and stars there?'

'Means he played brilliantly,' said Jilly, tired. 'Poetic. A metaphor.'

'Ah!' said Tai Pang. 'Metaphor. I understand. "Cultural waltz" is also metaphor, I think?'

'Yes,' said Jilly absently.

'But what means it?' said Tai Pang.

9

In March Abigail arrived from Canada, a high flier, an academic, on a six-week diagnostic mission. In her late forties, she had straight silver hair, beautifully cut, and chiselled features which snub-nosed Jilly envied. Abigail wore granny glasses and no make-up. Her routine, which comprised meetings with Chinese high-ups, hardly impinged on Jilly's but she was friendly and interested in people. Abigail's interpreter was Professor Zhang herself, junior only to the Principal. Abigail adopted Jilly as a sort of sister, a role Jilly was happy to play. They spent the evenings talking in Abigail's flat, so she could receive telephone calls from her husband, a minister of religion in Nonconformist Nova Scotia, and from their only daughter.

'Don't you wish you had a son?' said Jilly.

'Who's hung up on sons? I'm not Chinese.'

'What about your husband? A man expects to have a son,' said Jilly, whose father had never forgiven her for being a girl. She remembered Zhang's story and shuddered.

'People damage their daughters talking that way. I'm really proud of Laura. She works with MicMac native Americans on a reservation. What does your girl do?'

'Oh, she's married,' said Jilly evasively.

Abigail, by discipline a sociologist, was fascinated by the foreign community, especially Fox, who told her he was a freelance freedom fighter. She was making a study of textbooks used with Chinese students and interrogated him on his course contents. He confirmed that to Chinese people the word 'propaganda' had no negative connotations and that the current affairs textbook taught that in America official policy was extermination of Black and Red peoples, while rape was winked at as a means of control over women.

'And what nonsense do *we* believe about *them*?' Abigail asked Jilly.

'Try asking Gloria: she believes anything derogatory she hears.'

'You know she and Francine are an item?'

Jilly was not sure she believed this. 'They tell foreign men who come here that sex with Chinese girls is illegal, but it happens.' She was thinking of Fox and 'Miss Passport'.

'The authorities aren't very happy about Ben and the young teacher they call Miss Phoenix,' said Abigail.

'Ben? He's celibate,' said Jilly.

'They're planning to get rid of him just the same. They set the girls to look at his bed sheets. They suspect him because he's a "Western Marxist", unduly influenced by Maoism. And to the leaders here Maoists in the West are mere misfits and political vandals, stigmatized as "Loony Left". It is not wise to be too far to the Left in China today.'

'But he's brilliant, a marvellous teacher!'

'He's giving private coaching to that girl and they don't approve. He told me he'd never been a Party member, but he always analysed events from a Marxist-Leninist viewpoint. He said Marx never saw a lightbulb and offered no programme for the present. Communism had to evolve. Under Mao, he said, China was self-sufficient for the first time. Now she has to import millions of tons of grain.'

'The country wastes precious foreign currency on imported luxuries,' Ben had said. 'It's wicked. Mao has been betrayed.'

'What about the persecutions, the torture, the shootings, the awful things that happened to Zhang?' said Jilly.

'I said something like that and he said there could be no progress without evolutionary struggle, and he took the longer view,' said Abigail. 'I'm not sure I believe in progress.'

'Zhang's father had to wear a dunce's cap,' said Jilly.

Abigail wanted to know about the elderly women wearing red armbands who sat outside each housing block. Jilly explained they were there to report on antisocial or immoral behaviour.

'They're supposed to prevent fights by granny-power,' said Jilly, 'and literally pull people apart. Fighting is bad form, you see. All discussion is supposed to start with common ground, leaving the meat of the argument to the end. We think they waste time beating about the bush, and they think we are grossly impolite if we come to the point too quickly. To be aggressive is to lose face: I gather it's something to do with Chinese grammar and the topic sentence, but I'm out of my depth.' I'm Ben's pupil all right, she thought. 'We think they are woolly when they think they're being tactful,' she said.

'Somebody ought to tell Gloria.'

'We've all tried, goodness knows,' said Jilly. 'Gloria says we shouldn't pander to them. She accuses Fox of "going native", an expression one really can't use now, because he goes to Chinese bathhouses.'

'They think she's a joke,' said Abigail. 'She annoys them so they deal with it by laughing at her.'

'Until I came here,' said Jilly, 'I thought the distinction between shame cultures and guilt cultures was a fiction. But this is a shame culture all right: they don't seem to feel bad about telling lies or cheating, only about being found out and losing face. They have no still small inner voice, like we have.'

'You mean like people of our age have,' said Abigail. 'Young people, the ones who have lost religion, don't have it either. If they have a conscience, it's more likely to be a social one than a moral one. My daughter Laura is against the American dream, materialism and pollution.'

'We're all against pollution, aren't we, so long as our own jobs are safe?'

'She's living with a native American,' said Abigail.

Jilly said she had often wondered how it felt to be a Redskin, a historical leftover, under the heel of a foreign invader, no function in the lands stolen from you, all your traditional skills redundant, except for spidermen till they drank too much and fell off the scaffolding.

'He's not a spiderman,' said Abigail. 'He's got a Master's in ethnography and has a government grant to teach youngsters their own tribal lore. Canadian social policy isn't like the American melting pot. Our government pours money into ethnicity. Any group looking for roots can get a grant. Canada doesn't want minorities who miserably straddle two cultures and belong to neither. They're setting up universities for Inuit, where they can be taught in their own language. I don't approve, not because I'm prejudiced, but because they're not married. The congregation don't like it either. I've asked Dan to talk to her, but all he'll say is it's her life and he won't interfere. And him a minister! Suppose they have children?'

'Young people in China can't get married without permission from their work units, and they have to wait till their mid-twenties,' Jilly told Abigail. 'The IUD is the most common contraceptive, and only married women can be fitted with them. The pill has a bad reputation here, because they never moved on to the low-dosage one. The pill seems to be restricted as a means of social control. Not so long ago, I hear, Chinese girls were sentenced to corrective labour for sleeping with their boyfriends.'

'My daughter shacked up with her fellow at nineteen,' sighed Abigail. 'Restless, these young women, don't you think? They're mated but not breeding, and they're not happy, for all they're living in sin.'

'When I was a girl, the women's magazines and our mothers all told us to say no until safely married – '

'I did!' said Abigail.

'Now they give detailed instructions on technique. I read in one magazine how to get married within a year, a recipe, only they called it a game plan. It was everything we were told not to do: you should run after a man if you fancied him, telephone him, invite him to dinner in a restaurant, coax him into bed and not take no for an answer! Oh yes, it said, "Never sleep with a man until you've interviewed him for at least thirty hours". Going to the cinema didn't count as interviewing because you can't talk in the movies.'

'I remember a girl at college who thought she was ugly. She was just ordinary, really. She wanted to get engaged, so she invited him to supper, played sweet music, ate by candlelight, lashed out on a bottle of wine. She unbuttoned her blouse and he fled, leaving her to wash the dishes. Funny thing was, she boasted of it. Then there's all the garbage about reviving a flagging marriage with a new nightie.'

'I sometimes think they got it right in Israel, on kibbutz, bringing kids up in groups instead of with their parents.'

'Oh, they've stopped all that,' said Abigail. 'The children were all screwed up, like the ones in the hippy communes.'

'Is that so?'

'There's a considerable literature on it.'

'Would you like your daughter to marry this man?' said Jilly.

'I wouldn't choose it, but I could accept it more easily than the present situation,' said Abigail.

'China has more than fifty minority nationalities,' said Jilly. 'The Miao people have a lovely courtship ritual. Once a year they dress up, with singing and dancing, and the girls stand in twos or threes, and the men look them over. When a young man finds a girl he fancies, he asks her to marry him – but it's all done by singing. He makes it up as he goes along, about how beautiful she is and how he can't do without her. If the girl likes him, they exchange photographs. They've got gifts ready in advance and that's how they get engaged. It's true. I can think of worse ways of choosing a partner.'

'But Christian marriage is different from that,' said Abigail.

On a short stay, Abigail did not want to spend too much on setting up home, so borrowed. Gloria spent her evenings with Francine, so Abigail and Jilly cooked in turns, in Abigail's flat, using Jilly's gear, which had to be carried up and downstairs, because Abigail had to be at home for the phone calls from home which never came. Abigail shamed Jilly by scrubbing all the brown stains off her roasting tin.

'I'm lost without my dishwasher and microwave,' she said and grumbled at the sparseness of the shops. Jilly had got used to that.

'I thought you were Green,' teased Jilly. 'You can't be Green with a dishwasher. Water is short in this country.' She did not tell Abigail that she had recently washed up in a fierce liquid that took the surface off her cutlery. She took a second look at the squeezy bottle. It told her, in English as well as in Chinese that it was for cleaning stains from lavatories. Jilly was not a fanatical scrubber, like Abigail, but she was a careful rinser. Neither of them was poisoned.

Abigail was slightly anti-American, which surprised Jilly. Abigail explained that America forbade other countries to sell weapons or computers to China because they considered the Chinese market to be theirs. Canada was in competition with the USA.

'All the screaming about *Québec libre* is more economic than political. They want to break free of Canada so they can lock in more closely with the American economic system. Quebec is the centre of the North American arms industry. That's where all the Star Wars research went on before we heard anything about it. The Americans have four nuclear bases on the East coast of Canada. If we don't get our strike in first, then the Yankees plan to detonate all the mines in Halifax harbour, to kill us all before the Russians can do it.' She and Dan were pacifists, nuclear disarmers.

Like most newcomers to dusty Beijing, Abigail developed a sore throat. She was prescribed a herbal remedy that looked like a nut, but when boiled turned to jelly. She drank the liquid, as ordered, reddish brown and alkaline, and it worked. Jilly told her the medieval Anglo-Saxons had worshipped willow-bark, a natural source of aspirin. Jilly was drawn to alternative and herbal medicine. Professor Zhang warned them against uncritical faith in Chinese medicaments.

'Some of them contain mercury,' she said. 'Herbal medicine is better.'

Because Abigail was so grand, she was escorted by Zhang, who made a point of inviting Jilly along. Zhang took them to the Temple of Heaven, in the south of the city, where the emperors gave thanks for good harvests, with multiple gift shops. Abigail was a shopaholic, not for herself, though she dressed well, but for presents. Chinese paintings, some on paper, some on stones, jade boxes, carved animals, silks, cloisonné, kites, fans, red lacquer, trays, embroideries, painted figurines, a set of traditional Chinese musicians carved in onyx, Abigail swept them all up with her credit card.

Jilly was a penny-pincher rather than a shopper. She had forsworn shopping for clothes with Rosalind, who trailed from boutique to smart boutique, hesitating, dithering, contradicting herself, holding clothes against her body, trying them on, and asking solemnly, 'Do you think it suits me?' If Jilly said yes, Rosalind usually replied indignantly, 'But you *know* I can't wear this length/colour/neckline...' Jilly bought clothes mainly by price and had picked up bargains in charity shops. Self-decoration was with Rosalind a solemn ritual. Inevitably the new items were very much like the ones she had already: smart suits, soft sweaters, wide belts, heavy jewellery, beautiful shoes.

After a whole afternoon spent hunting through frivolous, ephemeral fashion, Rosalind always ended up with expensive classics, the mixture as before. Jilly wondered whether Clytie was helping Rosalind buy maternity clothes. Jilly had once asked Rosalind, 'Why don't you start with the shops you've bought from before and save all the traipsing about?'

'But the *schlepping* is what makes it fun!' cried Rosalind, opening her big dark eyes in amazement. 'I enjoy having a good poddle round till I know what I'm looking for.' Jilly's Methodist grandmother had said vanity was a sin.

Now Jilly watched Abigail collecting loot like a squirrel and wondered whether her own cheeseparing was the legitimate result of a penurious childhood and a studious youth, not to mention widowhood, or was it, as Clytie said, a neurosis? Hannah was another careful one. On the shopping bus she would gloat over a haul of beansprouts, boasting of having haggled the stallholder down.

When Abigail bought a jade and amber necklace ('Not for me, but my Laura will love it'), Zhang said sadly, 'My mother had one like that, but she threw it away when everything pretty was criticized as bourgeois. When I was in the countryside, the peasants criticized us for the way we spoke. Now the ultra-leftists are criticized. We students and intellectuals dumped on the farmers were a burden to them: unskilled, extra mouths to feed. If we were not rightists, why were we being punished?'

She regretted the way statues of Mao were being demolished or boarded up. 'True,' she said, 'he was a tyrant, but other tyrants are memorized. To destroy them is to destroy history. It was not a good time. Mao encouraged Chinese to have many children, so population doubled. What do you think of our one-child policy?'

'What do you think of it?' asked Abigail, unwilling to commit herself.

'Painful but necessary. No birth control policy can be too severe for us. But the duty to take care of parents is still Chinese tradition. The burden on only child is heavy. Soon nobody will have uncles or cousins.'

'Have you any children?' Abigail asked Zhang.

'No,' was all Zhang said. Abigail was horrified when Jilly told her Zhang's story.

'I should have been more tactful,' moaned Abigail.

'How could you have known? You can't be here long without hearing these terrible tales of woe. Zhang told me how people were punished for failing to preface every speech at meetings with: "As our great leader teaches us" and ending with a sort of doxology about Mao from whom all blessings flowed. It would be funny, except that people were persecuted. Millions were starved, or killed or they committed suicide. You don't have to ask questions. People like to tell you.'

Abigail's telephone rang.

'It'll be Dan!' she cried. After a minute she said, 'I have nothing to say to you!' and hung up.

'Oh, Jilly, it's an awful man who's trying to get me to smuggle Chinese antiques, the ones with the red seal, and Chinese ivories for a private buyer. He's been pestering me and he's even tempted Dan. Now he's turned up in China. I will not do anything illegal! He's been at me to get in touch with a crooked dealer he knows.'

'And have you?'

'Of course not! I've been buying tourist junk for friends and family. I wouldn't dream of breaking the law.'

'Why doesn't he buy the stuff himself if he's in the country?'

'He won't risk it and anyway he hasn't any money. He's always telling strangers that his wallet has been stolen. He's one of Dan's lame ducks. A minister, you know, has to help.'

'Help a crook?'

'I tell Dan it's all fool's gold. He's always had this pipedream of making a fortune through some brilliant *coup* other people can't match. He's got his doctorate, but he doesn't feel he's recognized as really smart on what he earns. It's a lot less than I do. And he's got this liberal guilt about French Canadians. He wanted me to cash in our life insurance policies, but I won't sign. He had the idea of taking out a loan with the house as collateral, but the house isn't ours; it belongs to the church. We need our insurance policies to buy somewhere to live when Dan retires. We don't have any risk capital. And now Dan tells me I'm selfish and shortsighted and have no vision and he's not intending to be poor for ever – Laura's education cost us a mint, I can tell you, and all her friends had brand-name clothes, and it was a struggle to keep ahead.

And Fabré's always closeted in with Dan, building castles in the air, while I'm working my butt off on an academic salary to keep the bills paid and put something aside and now this gosh darned awful man has followed me to China. Can I put a stop on phone calls?'

'Not really. There's no way of leaving messages, either.'

'Can we move into your flat in the evenings? He might ring again. I'll never forgive Dan for this, never. He's lost sight of the fact that Fabré's scheme is criminal.'

'Has Dan given him any money?'

'Only a handout at the beginning: a so-called loan when he'd so-called lost his wallet. Never got that hundred dollars back. Dan seems mesmerized by him. It's driving me crazy.'

The phone rang again. 'I told you I had nothing to say to you!' screamed Abigail.

'Abigail?' said Zhang's voice. 'I think there is a mistake. We are invited to a performance tomorrow...'

Jilly enjoyed the show. A conjuror, told to extinguish his cigarette, obeyed but drew one lighted cigarette after another out of the air. Two girls tied themselves in knots, did the splits while standing on their heads and stuck their faces between their own thighs. Two fat little gentlemen in brown suits imitated sounds from birdsong to motorbikes. A male dancer seemed to leap six feet into the air. Zhang said he received only a basic salary. Abigail said his talent would make him rich in the West.

'But he has privileges,' said Zhang. 'He has won prizes and is in *Who's Who of Artists in the Chinese People's Republic.* By the way, Abigail, there was a telephone call from your friend Fab Ray.'

'No friend of mine,' said Abigail through gritted teeth.

'The call came to the office and Professor Chong took it. This man says he came to Beijing from Shanghai by train and his wallet is stolen. He asked to borrow money.'

'I'm so sorry you've been bothered, Madame Zhang,' said Abigail, investing her with this all-purpose courtesy title.

A letter arrived from Dan in reply to Abigail's angry call to him. 'Fabré complains you have been no help to him in China. He is down on his luck. Show compassion.' A letter arrived from Fabré himself, which Abigail tore up unread.

Zhang asked Abigail and Jilly, who were paid partly in US dollars, to lend her some. 'Only for a few days. The money will be returned. One of our teachers is emigrating to the United States, and she must show she has enough dollars to survive there. We all help her, but my dollars are few.'

They lent the money without hesitation.

A few days later Dan rang to say his credit card had been stolen so Abigail couldn't use hers. Somebody had run up a bill for airline tickets and luggage before he missed it. He refused to suspect anybody in particular. Abigail borrowed from Jilly and bought Jilly a silk dressing gown embroidered with dragons. 'For your birthday,' said Abigail.

'But it isn't my birthday till the autumn!'

'Never mind,' said Abigail, who showered gifts on the Chinese.

'Why do you buy all these presents and nothing for yourself?' asked Jilly.

'The congregation will expect it and there's no pleasure like it.'

Abigail repaid Jilly's loan with a cheque but the Bank of China refused to honour it. They wanted a banker's draft, authenticated in Canada. Abigail promised to see to it as soon as she was home. Jilly trusted her.

Abigail wanted to take Zhang and Jilly out for a farewell dinner but didn't have the money. Having obtained permission from Mr Da, Zhang gave her an official banquet.

'If a Chinese person is your friend,' said Zhang, 'she is your friend for life.'

'And in England,' said Jilly.

'On the American continent,' said Abigail, 'the distances are vast and we move around. We make friends easily and forget them easily. Dan and I were planning a trip to Europe sometime, if we can afford it, after he retires, and it would be great to visit with you, Jilly. But you mustn't expect me to write.'

They discussed national diets.

'Is it true that in Europe you eat snail?' said Zhang.

'Yes, but horribly expensive,' said Jilly.

'Not poor people's food?'

'Not at all. Rich person's luxury.'

Zhang shuddered. 'To Chinese the notion of eating snail is disgusting,' she said, picking up a large gelatinous sea-slug in her chopsticks.

Jilly helped Abigail pack, filling several stout boxes. She bequeathed to Jilly vitamin pills, food, stamps.

'I'd rather have your company than your goods, Abigail. I shall miss you and the gossip.'

'That reminds me, they say that Hannah Wong is having an affair with that young man Fox,' said Abigail. 'She's spreading it around that you and I are lesbians. Not my bag.'

'Nor mine. But some feminists want to do without men altogether,' said Jilly.

'There seem to be two kinds of feminist: the ones like me, who believe in womanly ways, in nurturing and caring, and the others who want to be like men, flying fighter planes and the like.'

Dan telephoned to say there was a warrant out for Fabré's arrest but nobody knew where he was. 'He stole my wallet, too,' confessed Dan. 'I've been a fool.'

Zhang and Jilly accompanied Abigail to the airport. As the car drew away they heard a commotion on campus.

'Hu Yaobang, former leader, has died,' said Zhang. 'He was popular with students, but too radical to please government. He wanted too much change. Two years ago he was disgraced.'

Jilly and Abigail hugged at the barrier and Abigail disappeared into Customs with her excess baggage.

Riding back to the university with Zhang Jilly realized how lonely she had been before Abigail's arrival and would be again now she was gone.

Jilly had avoided saying so to Abigail the minister's wife, but she preferred Buddhist temples where the heathen in his blindness bowed down to wood and stone, to images of the tortured Christ. Candles and incense sweetly burned, the faithful knelt in prayer. Banned by Mao, they had returned to worship. The monks' faces were gentle, marked less by passion than by time. What madness, though, to imagine it pleased the gods to mortify the flesh! Ah, but what about the forgotten virtue of self-denial? Asceticism was not, as some said, a merely Christian mind-set. Societies swung between discipline and decadence. The Commonwealth had been followed by the Restoration and Mao had been more puritanical even than Cromwell. Mao had wanted China to outbreed the world. To go forth and multiply made sense for scattered nomad tribes; it was suicidal for a crowded modern world, as the present government in China recognized, despite murmurings from the professional and intellectual classes. Why had so many peoples been impelled to sacrifice their children to imaginary gods? Jilly had been brought up to look on religious evolution as a ziggurat, culminating in Christianity, though of course only Protestant nonconformity was true and free of superstition; the British government, legal system and constitution were the most mature and uncorrupted in the world, the envy of lesser breeds. Yet now people were saying one religion was as good as any other, and it was all right to have none at all. Jilly didn't have much, only sentimental memories of childhood Christmases.

Rosalind had once asked whether eating mince pies was a religious ritual. The notion made Jilly laugh, but it set her thinking that the boundaries between religious belief and social custom were unclear. The Chinese used the word 'spiritual' with a freedom Jilly found faintly embarrassing. She was careful to respect all foreigners, but in her heart, she asked herself, did she regard them, even distinguished scholars like Zhang, as equals? She hoped she did. Chinese people considered foreigners as rich and arrogant. It was difficult not to seem so, when she was so much better off financially than they were and she had something they wanted and deferred to: the English language, even if the young preferred the American version. Was she kind enough to Ming, so hardworking, so deferential? What were her real feelings about China? She was forced to admit that, despite spectacular exceptions, it seemed to her a drab, shabby country of secrets, of gates locked and guarded, of barbed wire. Jilly had a recurring dream in which the mysterious characters of Chinese writing resolved themselves into English words so she could read them. She had no key. She did not want to be a racist like Gloria, yet even Ben, self-confessed 'friend of China' and Marxist, was detached and analytical. Was it true that he had an emotional relationship, even a platonic one, with a Chinese girl? Jilly had no right to be jealous, but she had hoped that Ben, who was always doing his best to restrain Gloria, had a special friendship with herself. Perhaps it was his ecclesiastical training that made him friendly and benevolent to all, close to none. Rumour had it that he had gently rebuffed 'Miss Passport' when she called on him one night.

Puzzling these questions, Jilly fell asleep. She dreamed Rosalind gave birth to a monster. It chanted, over and over, 'My child is a wild child wild child my daughter Clytie mighty flighty Clytie naughty nightie' and Jilly woke convinced that this was a cosmic message of profound importance, which she must write down and pass on. When she tried to do so, the words had faded and she knew they signified nothing.

Hannah came round to ask for Jilly's help. 'I'm in love!' she announced.

'Yes?' said Jilly.

'Do me a favour. I let Bruce think I'm with you. If he calls and asks to speak to me, can you tell him I'll be right along, I'm in the bathroom or somewhere and give me a call in Fox's apartment, so I can call Bruce back from there.'

'I can't promise,' said Jilly. 'I may not be in every evening.'

Professor Chong sent a message to say the Xerox machine could not be used because there was no paper left. Jilly was exasperated as she wanted to copy worksheets. Grumpily she typed out her stencil, but was not allowed near the duplicating machine. Promised for Monday morning, the work was not ready when Jilly called for it. On Monday Jilly's classroom was unlocked but empty. Irritably she walked round campus and eventually found Mei Ling, who told her the students were on strike because girls at another university had been roughed up by police. Mr Da Feng and Professor Chong called a meeting of foreign teachers.

'You will go to your classes as normal. If nobody comes, you may leave. You must not involve with internal politics of China.'

Ben called a meeting in his flat. Miss Phoenix was with him. He said students were going on strike not only in Beijing's forty universities but in other major cities. Jilly read *China Daily* and listened to the BBC. She knew students were congregating in TianAnMen Square. By April 26 unrest had lasted a week and classes were officially suspended. Zhang and Mei Ling kept Jilly informed.

'The situation is serious,' said Zhang. '*Gongren Ribao*, the *People's Daily*, has published an important editorial. It must have been dictated by Deng Xiao Ping himself. It accuses the students of being an anti-communist rabble, egged on by a few counter-revolutionaries, troublemakers. It said crack troops are mobilised and warned that the government are not afraid of bloodshed.'

'All we want is an end to corruption, embezzlement and bribery,' said Mei Ling.

Ben said pedlars in the Square had been giving student protesters free food: they were not usually fond of students or intellectuals.

'The people are behind them,' he said.

Jilly could remember the Hungarian uprising, the Prague spring, teargas and water cannon in Warsaw. During her eight months in China, statespersons had arrived by the planeload: Rajiv, Benazir and George had all visited and appeared on TV with lidded cups of green tea. Now Mikhail was coming. Irina and Tanya were wildly excited. They boasted of being invited to a reception to meet him.

'Will you talk to him, do you think?' said Jilly.

Irina did not know: 'All they have told us is that we must be bee-yoo-ti-ful.'

'That won't be difficult,' said Ben courteously. Irina was a voluptuous blonde.

The shopping bus crawled through streets clogged with bicycles on their way to the square, banners, black, gold and geranium red braced on bamboo poles by cyclists in pairs. People spilled out of cramped hovels to applaud the demonstrators.

Tanya and Irina were fascinated: 'We have never seen this before. In our country we have no demonstrations.'

'You may have some now you're getting elections in the Soviet Union,' said Ben.

Irina did not think so.

Fox said that in America people always thought protests and demonstrations were the work of Communists; it was intriguing to see a march from inside a Communist country.

He started singing, 'Ho Ho Ho Chi Minh' and 'Mamama Mamama Mao Ze Dong'. Nobody took any notice.

'Those songs date you,' said Gloria.

People did their shopping as usual. Fox wandered off with his camcorder. Jilly got her hair done and had a manicure, intending to glam up a bit for the course for young teachers proposed by Zhang to fill the vacuum left by the student strike.

Zhang called to say the class was cancelled, as teachers were 'persuading students not to strike, but weakly'. Some teachers, too, were demonstrating.

'Is this another Cultural Revolution?'

'That was unusual,' said Zhang. 'At that time, intellectuals were not agitators but victims. Mao was bitter against intellectuals. He was born peasant, but wished to study at Beida, Beijing's top university. They refused him, only let him work in the library. Stalin cold-shouldered him, kept him waiting in the corridor for hours. He was a vengeful person, totally uneducated in the cosmopolitan sense: no foreign languages. Except for the Soviet Union, he never went abroad. Now we know he was a criminal. He wanted to keep the class struggle going for ever; now class struggle is out of date.'

Jilly remembered Abigail's remark that the middle class or bourgeoisie, villainous parasites in the Marxist mythology, were the meat in the sandwich, but she said nothing.

The spring was well advanced, the dreary streets transformed by tender leaf and frail blossom. Jilly went for solitary walks. The tailor and his wife shared their labour, the wife at the sewing machine while the husband pressed garments with a flat iron, the kind Jilly's neighbours at home used as doorstops. The child was now tied to the table leg. They formed a viable economic unit and unlike Hannah had a purpose in life. Their opportunities for malarkey must be nil.

Rosalind wrote to say Charles had been round to persuade Clytie to come back to him. She had refused. He had attacked her, attempting to strangle her. Rosalind telephoned the police but he was gone before they arrived. Clytie had refused to pursue the matter. Charles then made several abusive telephone calls. This time Clytie did complain and Charles was cautioned. He came again to Rosalind's flat, uttering threats. Clytie said she was going to divorce him as soon as possible. Oh dear oh dear, thought Jilly. But for the moment Clytie's problems were remote compared to student unrest in China. There was talk of a hunger strike.

10

'We have leisure! Let us go to the art gallery,' said Zhang. 'It will be quiet.' They took buses. The gallery was almost deserted.

'Chinese neglect their art galleries,' said Zhang.

Expecting the usual monotonous flowers, animals and scenery, Jilly was agreeably surprised by genre paintings in oils of Chinese rural life, portraits and still lifes. A large central canvas portrayed a group, heroes of the Long March. 'That's Agnes Smedley,' said Jilly. Zhang was impressed. She said she preferred realism in painting; it could be as symbolic as traditional art. 'But here is a special exhibition of traditional subjects: mountains, rocks, clouds, flowers, the vast forces of nature. Taoism is the foundation of our traditional painting. The artist is over there.'

Jilly smiled at him and said '*Ni hao*, hello' to him, adding '*Hen hao*, very good; *piao liang*, beautiful', which practically exhausted her Chinese vocabulary. Smiling back at her, he rose and gestured towards the visitors' book, handing her a writing brush.

'Like all Chinese artists, he is calligrapher as well as painter,' said Zhang. Jilly wrote 'Jilly, London' with the brush, apologizing for her clumsy strokes. The artist persuaded Zhang to take a photograph of him with Jilly on his camera. He told them, Zhang translating, that his exhibition was sponsored by the State Bureau of the Environment. Representing natural beauty, it was a protest against pollution. Jilly bought a few prints and agreed about the horrors of pollution. Smiles and handshakes were exchanged and the women left.

'Chinese artists must study many years,' said Zhang. 'They must immerse themselves in Chinese traditional culture, Chinese literature. All artists must be cultivated people. He is fifty, but looks young, isn't it? He has so many honours and distinctions, but remains modest and common.' Jilly realized that 'common' was a compliment. 'He says most people do not care about conservation. All they have interest in is how much money he earns. I think we should have asked him to sign the prints.'

'Let's go back,' said Jilly. They retraced their steps, but the artist was not available. They said he was at lunch. They found him perched on the colonnade in the sunlight, quietly munching a steamed bun. Joyfully he hailed their return and talked animatedly with Zhang. He wrote for Zhang, in elegant Chinese characters, 'We met by chance, but I hope this is not the end of our acquaintance.' Zhang explained it was a quotation from a classical Chinese poem. Ships that pass in the night, thought Jilly, savouring the moment. This would be something to tell Rosalind. On their way out, she paused to admire some stone pillars, wonderfully carved with grotesques, imps, animal and human figures. The artist said they had been found at Xian, the ancient capital, and used for tethering horses.

'Xian is an important archaeological site. There is much more there than terra cotta army,' said Zhang.

'So rich a skill for such a utilitarian purpose,' said Jilly.

'Perhaps too to keep away the evil spirits,' said Zhang. 'Country people believe they are everywhere. They believe in their heart the old gods are still alive.'

After the cool and peace of the gallery they were back in the city slipstream. High school pupils streamed past on their bikes towards the Square. On the flyover near the bus station a class of eight-year-olds in the red scarves of the Communist Young Pioneers cheered on truckloads of demonstrators, encouraged by their teachers.

They found a café selling cheap glass ornaments, tatty souvenirs and posters of female nudes. They ordered cool drinks.

'Yesterday,' said Zhang, 'the State Education Commission appealed to schoolteachers to prevent their pupils from joining the strike.'

'We couldn't prevent ours, could we? Why should schoolteachers do any better?'

'There is a rumour that we may have martial law. Do you think the world would condemn it?'

'Those with an interest in promoting Western-style multiparty democracy certainly would,' said Jilly.

'That sort of democracy would never be suitable for us,' said Zhang. 'We have been feudal for too long. We have progress, but it is sometimes the wrong sort. Do you think those pictures of women are progressive?'

'No,' said Jilly. 'They are decadent.'

Zhang said she was glad the protest was so peaceful. 'But what will happen to the hunger strikers? Will they die?'

Unable to do anything practical, the two women wandered round the shops. Jilly bought cotton shoes and a magnetic healer which promised relief from pain when rubbed on the affected parts.

'May I ask a favour? I am hot. May I come to your apartment for a bath and to wash my hair? Normally I go to the public bath house.'

It suddenly came home to Jilly that Zhang's flat had a lavatory and basin but no bath or shower.

'Why didn't you ask me before?' said Jilly, feeling all the guilt of unearned privilege.

'I had no right,' said Zhang, 'but today you have shared something important with me.'

Borrowing Jilly's electric hairdryer she mentioned that she had owned one herself, an electrical luxury bought after her visit to Britain, but it had broken down and was too expensive to replace.

'I'll leave this one behind when I go home,' said Jilly.

'But it is too expensive! You must take it home with you,' said Zhang.

Jilly explained that the plug would not fit in England and voltages were different. She persuaded Zhang to stay for supper.

Next morning a message came from Mr Da to say that showers were to be fitted in the foreigners' flats and there might be some slight inconvenience. He asked them to be patient.

Zhang came to see Jilly a few days later. 'Four thousand students, twenty from this university, are on hunger strike,' she said. 'They made their wills before they start and parents are pleading with the government, saying: "Save our children." Students threaten to burn themselves if their demands are not met. They want open debate with the government and they want it on television. They want nothing to do with the official student representative body. They want a new student committee and they want it recognized. Everywhere posters with witty slogans arc saying Deng Xiao Ping should resign. Xiao Ping means "Little bottle" and everywhere students are smashing little bottles.'

'What really happened in Xian, when students rioted and looted?' said Jilly.

'That was police in plain clothes,' said Zhang, 'to discredit the students. Most students say the premier, Li Peng, is incompetent and now the Party Secretary, Zhao Ziyang, has contradicted the editorial in the *People's Daily*. According to Zhao the student movement is patriotic. But it has been said that the students are behaving illegally and even Zhao has not yet said the protest is legal. Everywhere in China the constitution allows peaceful demonstration, but everywhere byelaws forbid it. Let us take water and succour our students.'

On their way out they met several students on bikes, who said they were guarding the hunger strikers in shifts. Mei Ling was among them.

'Your collar is grimy,' Zhang told him. 'You should wash it.'

'I am not in bed for much days,' said Mei Ling.

Zhang sent a message of support and said they were coming to visit.

'Give them my love,' said Jilly. Jilly lent the boy her camera.

All three gave the victory sign, a widespread gesture at that time. The two women travelled by bus and underground to the Square. The streets were clogged by demonstrators on bicycles. Zhang pointed out lawyers and bankers, engineers and diplomats, hotel workers and doctors, journalists and taxi drivers, teachers Chinese and teachers foreign, all marching with their students. Headbands carried a quotation from the revered writer Lu Xun: 'If we explode in silence, we die.' Instead of the usual brutal shoving, people smiled and stood back for one another. Instead of using elbows, they embraced. Money was put into student collecting boxes. Jilly thought it must have been like that in the Blitz.

'It is a really popular movement,' said Zhang, excited.

By the time they reached the Square they were both sweaty, tired and hungry. Under a hot blue sky, 30 degrees, many Chinese, distrustful of treacherous May weather, still wore thick woollen sweaters and padded trousers. Zhang and Jilly wore jeans and cotton shirts.

'Shall we go straight to the Square or shall we eat first?' said Zhang. They went to Kentucky Fried Chicken, which faced the giant Mao portrait across milling crowds. Clean and comfortable, the KFC restaurant was popular, though expensive. Jilly slipped Zhang a fifty-yuan note and let Zhang fetch the food.

'The girl at the counter saw you,' said Zhang, laying down the loaded tray. 'She said I should pay the 50 per cent surcharge on foreigner, so I told her I was treating you. Is it all right?'

'Of course.' Jilly was used to such juggling. They drank Pepsi and tucked into their spiced chicken.

'Normally,' said Zhang, wiping her fingers, 'I don't like chicken, but this is a real treat. Oh dear, Jilly. Here we are, stuffing ourselves in here, and just outside students are starving themselves to death for freedom, ready to die for a principle...' She put down her bun, eyes full of tears.

'Going hungry ourselves won't help them,' said Jilly. 'We need to keep our strength up for when students come back to class.'

They finished eating and went out into the broiling sun to join the million people in the Square. Tents and fluttering banners made it look like a medieval battle encampment. Television cameras were everywhere to greet Gorbachev but he was received indoors instead. Outside all was orderly, peace and love. Paths were cleared for the ever-growing parade. Banners accused the government of having iron hearts, of being geriatric bunglers; a broken and bleeding heart emblematized the Chinese people. Applause greeted a bandaged figure, gagged and blindfolded. Demonstrators smiled on the crowds, who waved to them in blessing. Bliss was in that dawn to be alive, to be young was very heaven, thought Jilly, stimulated but with a faint chill at the heart. Slogans were chanted, ambulance sirens howled as medics ran through the orderly lanes with students on stretchers. Otherwise there was little noise. Everybody was taking photographs. People with notebooks tried to interview hunger strikers, but they were ringed with ropes, bicycles and students with linked arms. An outer circle of sentinels, kindly but stern young men wearing headbands, patrolled, protecting them.

Zhang said to Jilly, 'They hold hands because their leaders have forbidden weapons, even pen-knives.' She used her professorial work-card, and eventually they got through, though she had to promise not to stay more than five minutes because the hunger strikers were exhausted. It was late afternoon and looking for their own students among so many was impossible. Emaciated to begin with, hunger strikers lay listless on their bedrolls, many refusing even water, though there was plenty about. Some smoked, some read; others kneaded icebags to cool their skinny wrists. A starving boy offered Jilly a cold facecloth to mop her dripping brow. She accepted, smiling. *Morituri te salutamus*, she thought.

'When did you last eat?' she said.

'Sunday.'

'But it's Wednesday now! How long do you intend to go on?'

'Until we win.'

'But you have brains, education, a future. China needs you.'

'We have no other hope.'

'Don't throw your life away, please don't do it!'

'Perhaps my country needs martyrs. I no longer want food.'

His shirt said, 'Give me liberty or give me death'. Jilly took his wasted hand between hers and pressed it. A man with a camera came up and motioned her to do it again. Jilly told him to get lost. Even in England protesters were routinely photographed by police. Encouraged by the support of Zhang and even more by that of her foreign friend, the boys handed them felt tips, imploring signatures on their caps and T-shirts. Jilly was touched but nervous. She didn't want her name found on the clothing of a dissident when the authorities reined them in, as she expected them to eventually. She wrote not her name, but just 'Good luck'. The young patriots smiled shyly, sweetly. Zhang, in tears, hugged them all.

'We have overstayed,' she said to Jilly. 'We cannot find our students. We may as well drink the water we are carrying, since these are refusing. Their health is endangered.' They drank the water they had brought. It was tepid.

The underground station at the city's splendid south gate was closed so they walked to the next. Zhang said the day had been inspiring. Jilly was moved but not hopeful.

Jilly longed for coffee, but none was to be had. They boarded a hot, crowded bus, after a long wait, and returned to campus. Electricity was turned off, so there was no bath or shower; the bathroom and kitchen were full of red dust and of Chinese plumbers, who always worked in threes, two doing the job, another watching. The *fuyuyuan* were sitting in her living room presumably to see that the plumbers didn't steal anything. One of the girls was reading Jilly's current letter to Rosalind, left in the typewriter Zhang had lent her. Jilly went next door to see if she could use Gloria's bathroom, but her apartment too was full of workmen and Gloria was out.

A heavy thunderstorm brought mud to the Square and with ankle-deep litter it became a health hazard. Doctors said strikers, without food for a week, would have no resistance to infection. Still people were pouring into Beijing to demonstrate and teachers went on drawing their salaries without working. Asian students at the Language Academy planned a token hunger strike in sympathy.

'The government must listen,' said Zhang, repeating the current mantra.

'Or arrest us as agitators,' said Jilly drily.

'We will protect you,' said the woman who had spent years as a manual labourer for the crime of being an intellectual.

'Thank you,' said Jilly, inwardly sceptical.

The students were disappointed in Gorbachev. They had hoped for his support, but all he would say was that they must not expect too much too soon. His visit was upstaged by the peaceful, disciplined 'turmoil'. He and the authorities had lost face. It was May and cherries, strawberries and marrows appeared on market stalls. Much of Jilly's time was spent with Chinese people who dropped in to tell her excitedly what was happening. The students explained they were on strike not against Jilly but the system. They believed the high-ups and their children held numbered Swiss bank accounts, and had air tickets for Switzerland in case the government fell. Ming apologetically came to watch the TV news. Seeing starving Ethiopians on the box she wondered why Africa seemed always poor and miserable. Jilly thought the same of China but did not say so. Weeping mothers broadcast appeals to the government to give in and prevent their children from starving to death. A student in pyjamas harangued Li Peng, blaming the government for overpopulation and economic underdevelopment. Jilly did not see how, when the one-child policy was enforced and marriage delayed, the government could be held responsible for overpopulation .

'What do you usually do? Do you go out in the evenings?' asked Jilly.

'We do not go out much,' said Ming. 'Courting couples go out. Others are too tired. They watch television. But I do not have television.'

TV news said students had called off the hunger strikes after a week, but persisted in occupying the Square. Government figures had visited them and warned that anarchy would not be tolerated; the demands were unrealistic, said the authorities. Deng Xiao Ping suggested forcibly removing all protesters to hospital, which the students treated as a joke.

'Li Peng is not to be trusted,' said Ming. 'His eyebrows go up in the middle like Chinese figure eight, an unlucky number. Shows bad character,' she said.

Ming told Jilly Ben was spending more and more time with Miss Phoenix. Jilly only said, 'Really?'

'He takes her into foreigners' canteen and watches she eats enough. Is it true Mr Fox is a spy?'

'I don't think so.'

'He has many girlfriend, I think,' sighed Ming.

'Yes. I don't think he's looking for a wife just yet,' said Jilly gently.

'I have nice cousin,' said Ming, 'but to marry cousin is forbidden. In the mountains, many births are illegal by incest. Children of cousin deaf, blind, cripple, sick in head.'

'Our Queen and her husband are cousins, second cousins anyway, and their children are all right.'

'I don't believe it,' frowned Ming. 'We have fifty million handicap people, all because people had children with cousin.'

The new showers, designed to switch on in the kitchen and to operate in the bathroom, could not be made to work. There was no hot water. Gloria called a meeting but nobody turned up. The foreigners washed in cold water and got used to it. The weather stayed warm.

Rosalind wrote to say that Clytie's husband, Charles, had been found at the bottom of the tower block where he lived. He was believed to have fallen off the balcony. There would be an inquest. Jilly felt she ought to send Clytie a letter of condolence but had no idea what to say. She wrote to Rosalind instead.

11

Martial law was declared on May 22. Jilly heard the news on her radio. 'Listening to rumours' had become an offence overnight, so Jilly went out hoping to hear some. It was forbidden to go to the Square and there were no buses or taxis. Truckloads of people defiantly streamed with their banners into town, while the rest waved encouragement. Even the tailor at the south gate shut up his one-room home workshop to come out on the street with his wife and child. Returning to campus, Jilly met Fox on his bicycle. He told her the Embassies had been telephoning their nationals and warning them that under martial law anybody could be shot on sight without redress.

'We're all ordered to stay indoors, or at least on campus.'

'Which *is* your Embassy, Fox? Do you hold a British passport?'

'Oh yes. They asked me to pass the message on to you. I left a note under your door. We must be ready to leave the country at short notice.'

'Where are you off to now?'

'I'm looking for action of course! I can make a fortune if I can get some good shots with this.' He patted his camcorder.

'You might get shots of a different kind,' warned Jilly. He pedalled rapidly away in his scarlet leather jacket.

Time dragged. 'Nothing seems to be happening,' Zhang reported. 'Students are still in the Square.'

Fox went missing. Hannah was distraught. 'Oh Judas Priest,' she wailed. 'If anything happens to him I'll just die. He means everything to me. Bruce is so withdrawn and unemotional I could scream. He says I live on my nerves. I've tried to persuade him he needs therapy but he never *listens*. Do you think Fox'll marry me if Bruce and I divorce?'

Jilly thought Hannah stood more chance than Ming, but Fox did not seem to her to be a marrying man. He was one of life's clowns, needing perpetual carnival. Ming pined for him. Jilly fancied him. Hannah adored him. Hannah kept coming back to pour out her woes. Jilly felt sorry for her so tolerated her in small doses. Hannah was not happy with Bruce, who was not her first husband. She had married to get away from her stepfather but Hannah's first husband was a gambler so they had divorced and Hannah had started right over and gone to college, prised Bruce away from his wife and married him.

'I thought having a baby would solve everything,' she moaned.

'It never does,' said Jilly.

'I'm still only thirty. I have a right to develop my potential.'

Jilly wondered what Hannah's potential might be. She was enviably good-looking. She left Reuben with one of the Chinese girls for hours at a time.

'What I want from life, really,' she said solemnly, 'is to have fun, just to have fun. Fox is a fun person.'

Jilly imagined the pair of them running naked through the streets in Rio and smiled.

'I went to look for my father,' Hannah said solemnly, 'and I guess Bruce is something of a father-figure for me, but that didn't work out, with my father I mean, because he married this gross woman, really awful, you can't imagine, and I never finished college because I fell pregnant and that's why I can't work here. I've been getting sick, terrible migraines, Bruce gives me no sympathy; he, like, I have to make my own niche. I'm still paying off my student loan. We haven't got a proper home anywhere. We're all just drifters here, academic flotsam, only I haven't even got the excuse of being academic.'

'China does collect misfits and oddballs,' said Jilly.

'Bruce wants me to take Reuben back to the States, because this country isn't healthy at present. If I go I'll have to take Reuben to my mother and her god-awful husband, a real SOB. I hear the airport is closed. If the planes don't fly, then I can't leave, can I?'

Tanks ringed the city. 'The people are still in control,' everybody said. 'If the demonstrators can hold on another day or two Deng Xiao Ping and Li Peng will fall.'

'Deng Xiao Ping has gone to Wuhan.'

'No, he's gone to a small garrison town somewhere.'

'It can't last: he's bound to fall like Humpty Dumpty.'

'The tourists are all tickled pink.'

'Either the country destabilises or we shall live under a military dictatorship,' said Ben. 'Resignation is not a tradition in China. He'll only go if the army turns against him.' He went everywhere with Phoenix, saying she was his eyes and ears. They walked hand in hand, a couple.

Buses and taxis reappeared and life went on as before. People poked their heads above the parapet, pooh-poohing danger. Students went on boycotting classes. Ming told Jilly that the People's Liberation Army, in tears, had refused to obey their generals. Provincial authorities protested against martial law. At an earlier rising, she said, the thirty-eighth division, the most feared in China, had been sent to quell rebellious students, but desisted when the students, who had done compulsory army training, started singing ' their songs'.

'Ah yes,' said Jilly wickedly. 'Orthodoxical revolutionary songs. I have heard of them.'

'After all,' said Ming, 'there are only three hundred thousand soldiers. What is that to a billion people?'

'But the army have weapons,' said Jilly. 'The people are unarmed.'

'If the tanks roll people will lie down in front,' said Ming. 'Grandmothers are ready to sacrifice lives for the young.'

Zhang told Jilly, 'Tanks may crush a few hundred people, but they cannot quell a whole population. There are too many of us for that.'

Ben predicted civil war. 'Phoenix says Zhao Ziyang's troops are on their way to the city. They say that he, like Brutus of old, has proscribed his two sons for corruption, but was outvoted by the hardliners. Li Peng has taken over as Party Secretary.'

Xiao Xu came to see Jilly.

'Have you been to the Square?' she demanded.

'Yes, I have.'

'And did you cry?' said Xiao Xu.

Jilly nodded.

'Then you are one of us,' said Xiao Xu, flinging her arms round Jilly, who was taken aback, knowing that to Chinese nostrils she smelt like strong cheese.

It was now illegal for Chinese people to listen to the BBC or Voice of America. People went on listening. 'How else,' they said, 'can we get reliable news?' Martial law was treated as a joke. The Square was barricaded by the people. Jilly's typewriter needed a new ribbon so she went to her office to type a letter to Rosalind. She wrote:

'Ming came yesterday. She goes out every night to put up barricades to keep soldiers out of the city. She believes that the army occupying the Forbidden City next to the Square are not there to control the students but to check the moderates in the Party. Zhao Ziyang has not been seen lately. Wan Li, who stood up for the protesters, has come back from Canada and was detained in Shanghai, supposedly on account of his health though his doctor is here in Beijing. He's back in Beijing now, having signed a recantation. You say you've seen our demos on TV. You can't imagine the heat, the sweat, the emotion...'

In came the librarian, Lao Wang, in his usual Mao suit, giving the victory sign. '*Tamen bu nung lai!* They can't come in,' he said excitedly. He mimed student resistance, pushing against an imaginary wall, confident that democracy, whatever that meant to him, was winning.

Every campus had its Democracy Wall where people gathered for news. They said the soldiers, forbidden to listen to radio or read newspapers, did not know they were in Beijing. When it was explained to them they had been sent to oppress the people, they reversed their trucks and retreated, always in tears; people said that they were not being fed except by generous Beijingers, and so had sworn never to hurt the citizens. A rough map appeared, showing access routes by which the tanks might enter the city, the nightly barricades of bikes and old bedsteads marked in red. Li Peng was caricatured with human head and snake's body. The mood remained euphoric, festive. People dressed in their best and hung about the streets; babies in frilled bonnets slurped icecream. Trains brought in protesters from the provinces and taxi fares quadrupled. Photography was banned and everybody took pictures. The mails stopped.

'We're incommunicado,' said Gloria.

'No, the mail is just slow,' said Ben.

'Do you think they'll seal the country off?'

'Too many foreign contracts,' said Ben.

The airport was said to be 'closed' but when it emerged that only domestic flights were cancelled Bruce Wong took his wife and child to the airport and sent them home.

Peasants in blue cotton clothes and wide straw hats were selling watermelon slices, like green boats. With their bright red inner flesh like gums and sharp points they looked oddly carnivorous, like crocodile jaws. The crisis had apparently fizzled out. People became bored and irritable.

Although there were still no classes, Fu Bing was anxious about his dissertation, on Thomas Hardy's *Tess*. He wrote that the novel showed 'combative consciousness'. Tess's fate symbolized the brutality of nineteenth-century capitalism and demonstrated that according to the doctrine of Christian a bastard could not be buried after death. The novel symbolized Darwin and Schopenhauer. Jilly gently suggested that the novel could also be seen in terms of class conflict, the peasant girl victim of Angel's bourgeois priggishness, while Alec did indeed represent capitalism. I sound like a member of a Marxist Feminist Collective, banging on like this, she thought.

Ming's face was trodden on in a scuffle at the barricades. Jilly visited her. She heard that Ming was threatened with expulsion from the Party. Party members who had marched or manned barricades were under orders to deny it.

'If I am expelled,' wept Ming, 'how can I ever marry? I love the Party. But now is time for reform. When we ask reform they say no. How can the government tell lies?'

'Governments everywhere get plenty of practice,' said Jilly.

'What is to happen next?' said Ming. 'Student leaders do not know what to do. It is symbolic to stay in the Square, but perhaps it has served its purpose?'

Overnight an eight-foot polystyrene statue was placed defiantly opposite Mao's portrait in the Square. She was called the Goddess of Democracy. The government said that if she was not demolished within twenty-four hours she would be taken down by force. It rained and damp students sang patriotic songs and chainsmoked. Zhang grew nervous.

'What about our students' careers?' she fretted. 'Maybe all colleges will be closed again for five years.'

Mei Ling returned Jilly's camera. He translated student chants for her:

'If Li Peng won't cut his throat
Students go on rocking boat;'

and

'If Deng Xiao Ping won't go away
We'll go to TienAnMen every day.'

He sighed. 'China gives young people no chance to fulfil themselves,' he said mournfully. 'If there is no hope to make things better, we become lazy and apathetic. For my own spiritual development I must study alone. Under socialism, nobody listens to the people. In Britain what happens if people protest?'

'We might have a general election,' said Jilly.

'In democracy, government must obey the people.'

'Yes and no,' said Jilly.

'I am discouraged,' said Mei Ling. His perm was growing out. 'You can go home. I have no escape. Deng Xiao Ping says foreigners do not understand complexity of China problems. You must tell the West what you have seen here – how we live, how poor we are. Tell them, and maybe we receive help.'

'Is there any hope of your coming back to class?'

'No. The Goddess of Democracy has been parted, I mean she is broken. They say arrest is begun. Government pay farmers ten kwai each to demonstrate in favour of martial law and there is to be a purge of the Party. All must write a self-criticism.'

No wonder Ming had been so upset.

'Will Deng Xiao Ping write a self-criticism, do you think?'

'Of course not,' said Mei Ling. 'He is a god, is he not? We have a saying, "As poor as a PhD, as bad as a Party member". We shall rise again. Then we shall be stronger.'

Still students poured into the capital. Telephone lines were overloaded. Anxious parents turned up on campuses to check that their children had not starved themselves to death. Jilly heard that a straggling rump of students were sitting in the Square in flimsy nylon tents, without water, food or money.

Jilly was unclear what the students meant by 'democracy' but she believed their dreams were futile. The protest would be crushed, like the miners' strike in Britain. The miners had been bloodied in pitched battles with police. So far the Chinese 'turmoil' had been practically bloodless. Jilly went for a walk on campus. June 3 was Children's Day. Jolly celebrations took place on the tennis courts. Music blared, children in uniforms ran races, happy, laughing, watched by adoring parents. The little girls had painted lips, cheeks and nails, a spot of lipstick on each forehead, a fashion copied from Indian films. Jilly rejoiced in the freedom of their little feet. In previous generations the bones would have been crushed with a heavy stone and bound. Zhang had once said, to Jilly's horror, 'My grandmother had bound feet; her way of walking was so pretty!' The first time Jilly saw an old woman hobbling with a stick on three-inch feet, she wept. Later she got used to seeing them. Footbinding was made illegal in 1912, when China became a republic. But, as Ben had explained to Jilly, parents went on doing it, afraid that big-footed daughters would never find husbands.

A little girl in one of the frilly frocks beloved of Chinese mothers, layered in scarlet net, was climbing a gate, confidently, unchecked, like a gaudy butterfly clinging to a stalk. Jilly hoped she was a lucky emblem, and took a photograph.

Zhang laid on a party that evening. She invited Professor Chong, Ben, Phoenix, Bruce Wong, Gloria, Francine, the Russians and Jilly. She had coaxed Ming into coming. They tucked into fish, chicken, pork, bean-curd, sliced tomatoes in sugar, steamed buns, eggplant, all in spiced gravies full of monosodium glutamate. Zhang told stories of foreign teachers: of the beauty who had put her feet on the desk, of an American man who was always late, taught nothing and made passes at girl students.

'He invited me to his apartment and when I made excuse, he offered money!'

'Did he get the sack?'

'We never break a contract,' said Zhang.

'But we are supposed to behave ourselves,' said Jilly. 'In Britain a man who behaved like that would lose his job. He insulted you. Didn't you complain?'

'It would have been embarrassing,' said Zhang. 'Foreign teachers are temporary.'

They spoke of Clifford Odets and 'George Shaw'. Ming wondered was it true that Shakespeare was really great. They compared family life in different countries.

Zhang said that when she was a child four generations lived together in a twelve-room house.

'Much quarrels, I think,' said Ming.

'Now people have their child early, so they can have bigger room. We have over six million families waiting for housing. Living space averages just over six square metres. We have six hundred and fifty thousand households crowded in shelters offering less than two square metre for each person,' recited Chong.

The others wondered how he held such figures in his head.

Francine wondered whether all Chinese women wanted children.

'Yes,' said Ming. Her black eye was fading.

'Some younger women do not want responsibility of providing grandchildren,' said Phoenix. 'They hope a sister or sister-in-law will do it for them. But soon there will be no sisters, no sisters-in-law.'

'China is run by geriatrics,' said Chong. 'Why do progressive governments become reactionary when they gain power? I thought,' he said gloomily, 'of joining one of the democratic parties, but they are useless. They sit on the People's Congress, but that is only a rubber stamp for the Central Committee, and the Central Committee rubber-stamps decisions made by the Politburo.'

Bruce Wong spoke of being an American citizen in a Chinese body. He was friendly, amusing. Jilly wondered whether his reclusive habits were a defence against Hannah's demands. What could it be like, married to somebody so self-centred? Did Bruce know or care about Hannah and Fox? Jilly was intrigued. She warmed to him: he was attractive. Zhang politely accompanied the foreigners back to their compound. It was rude, in China, to leave guests at the door. To honour them, you walked to their homes, or at least to the bus stop. It was a beautiful warm night. The sodium lights bleached the leaves, velvety against a green sky. It might be good, they agreed, to organize a trip to the Mongolian grasslands by train, to ride Mongolian horses and sleep in yurts.

As they entered the campus gate they heard the student broadcasting service abusing Deng Xiao Ping. They went back to their flats. Jilly was thinking Chong was less of a stuffed shirt than she had imagined. She started to write a letter to Rosalind. The telephone rang.

'The night is young,' said Bruce Wong. 'Do you feel like more partying? I do.' He arrived with a bottle.

'I thought you only liked playing chess with your computer,' said Jilly.

'I play other games, too,' he said. 'Political tension is aphrodisiac. Don't you find it so?'

12

Fast asleep when the telephone rang, Jilly was surprised to find a Chinese man beside her in a too-narrow bed. Her head ached. Drowsily she answered.

It was Rosalind, choking and seemingly hysterical.

'Where's the fire?' said Jilly crossly. 'It's six o'clock on Sunday morning.'

She was still sleepy. Bruce smiled at her and stroked her arm.

'Haven't you heard?' shrieked Rosalind.

'Is Clytie all right?'

'Clytie's fine. Do you really not know what's happened?'

'Spit it out, for God's sake,' grumbled Jilly .

'It's Saturday night here and we've seen it all on television.'

'Seen what on television?'

'TienAnMen Square! Forty-two killed, a hundred injured – '

'Bloody, bloody fools,' said Jilly, over and over again. She burst into tears. 'Bruce, they've killed people in the Square – '

'Bruce? Who's Bruce?'

'Oh Jesus,' said Bruce, American, pulling on his clothes.

'A friend. Never mind. Tell me what's going on.'

'A man stood in front of a tank. We saw it on the news. Do take care, Jilly. Clytie wants a word.'

'Mum, are you coming home?'

'I don't know,' said Jilly. 'It's a shock, but we all sort of expected it. They may cancel the planes or cut off the telephones soon. I love you, Clytie. Are you all right?'

'Love you too, mum. I may go back to university. Rosalind says you can come here until the Japs are out of your house. I – '

The line was cut. Jilly collapsed in tears.

'There's an old Chinese saying: "The water of pain puts out the fire of joy",' said Bruce.

There was a knock at the door. Jilly grabbed a dressing gown. It was Ben, with Phoenix. She was in tears and wore a black armband. Jilly invited them in and made tea. Phoenix had been listening to the student broadcasts. A headless female body had been identified as Xiao Xu. Weeping girls, pleading with soldiers for their lives, had been bayoneted and shot. Teargas had been used. Injured students had been taken not to hospital but to jail. Spectators had been machine-gunned.

All that day Chinese and foreigners wept in each other's arms. Crowds gathered at Democracy Wall, with its paper memorial wreaths and photographs of mangled bodies and crushed bicycles. Professor Chong checked the dorms and reported that, as well as one slaughtered student, five more were missing.

'This is a terrible day,' said Chong, 'the last desperate bite of maddened dogs. They have shot old people, students and workers.' Outside the campus walls shooting was incessant, vehicles were set ablaze and helicopters clattered overhead. A stunned mother carried on to campus the dead body of her nine-year-old son, with seven bullet wounds in him, and laid him, weeping, at the foot of Democracy Wall. 'Look what they have done to the children!' she cried. The child had peered out of a window.

'It could easily have been Reuben,' Bruce kept saying. He was trying to phone Hannah to say he was still alive. 'Communism and fascism show the same face.'

'Are you still a Marxist, Ben?' said Jilly.

'Oh yes.'

'After this?'

'It's barbaric, but a mistake like this doesn't negate the truths of Marxist-Leninism any more than the Inquisition invalidates the truths of Christianity,' said Ben.

'How can you say that?'

'I follow the dictates of my own heart,' said Ben, his arm round Phoenix.

Jilly felt the need to make some ritual gesture of grief, wishing she could light a candle or even cross herself without feeling foolish. Alice volunteered to console Xiao Xu's parents, who lived nearby. Ming asked to use Jilly's telephone. She was worried about her brother. Jilly gave Ming the key to her flat.

Gloria made enquiries about getting to the airport but had been told the only chance was a pedicab or bicycle taxi. Mei Ling and three of the missing students returned to campus on their bicycles, their shirts splashed with blood. He said bodies were being scooped off the ground and dumped in Army trucks. He carried with him the bloodied hard hat of a worker bayoneted to death. Other students brought spent bullets and teargas canisters. The watchers formed a guard of honour for them and applauded.

Ming, unable to get through to her brother's university by telephone, queued for two hours at the Post Office to send a telegram to her parents, letting them know she was still alive. Two soldiers, she reported, had been stoned to death just outside the campus gates. She set off on her bicycle to find her brother, but came back again when she found the road blocked by blazing trucks. Corpses lay in the streets. The sound of shooting continued all day. Bruce and Jilly did not venture out. The phones were still working but the operators were constantly engaged and, when they weren't, allowed callers only three minutes apiece. People said the news was spreading by word of mouth.

The Ayatollah Khomenei died the same day as Xiao Xu, but Jilly only heard about it later. Chinese TV showed a tantalisingly brief newsflash of the demolition of the Goddess of Democracy and soldiers sweeping up litter in the Square, no students or blood in sight. A talking head announced that a great victory had been won against counter-revolutionary vermin and that the previous year's had been a bumper harvest. A radio newsreader announced that a crime had been committed against the Chinese people. He was interrupted by military music. Rumour said he had been dragged away from his microphone and shot, like the petty embezzlers whose punishment was recorded on the regular news and whose names were posted at railway stations with red ticks denoting execution.

At attack on the universities by soldiers was expected. The student broadcasting station was hastily dismantled. Phoenix, Ming and students were sitting in Ben's flat, unofficial foreigners' HQ. Everybody wore black armbands.

'We can't let you go back to your dorms tonight,' said Ben. 'Stay here with us.'

'If we stay here after ten o'clock,' said Mei Ling, 'we shall be expelled.'

'If you go back, you may be killed. Perhaps we can give you a little time.'

The Chinese boys and girls went out of the foreigners' compound, clocking out at the guardhouse and creeping back upstairs under cover of darkness. Ming, Phoenix and the girls went with Gloria, Francine, Alice and Jilly, the boys with Ben and Bruce.

'If I die intercepting a bullet,' said Alice, 'I shall have died bearing witness to Christ Jesus. And by the way, Jilly, I forgive you about my fork.'

'This is no time to be worrying about forks, Alice.'

It was agreed the foreigners would stay up to keep watch while the visitors doubled up two and three to a single bed. Carefully Jilly sat with the lights turned off and avoided showing herself at the window as she cautiously peered out. It was a moonlit night and the gunfire had stopped. Jilly had ice in her stomach. Kiss your nerves goodbye, the horror movie poster had said. The blood today had been real. Yet Jilly, although alert, felt strangely anaesthetized against fear. She half expected the door to be kicked down. If it were, she would surely be shot with the rest, for the authorities would not want witnesses. She hoped that if death were coming it would be by bullet and not by bayonet. She was even slightly excited, with an adrenalin rush. We are programmed for danger, she thought: now I understand people who enjoyed the war. Fear of death made her feel intensely alive. I'd rather die a heroine of the Resistance than as a collaborator, she thought: then mocked her own heroics. At four o'clock she squeezed in with Phoenix and another girl and slept fitfully till about nine. The girls, after sharing Jilly's oat porridge, insisted on washing the dishes and making the twin beds, thanked Jilly politely and went back to their dorms.

Chinese people came and went, asking the foreigners what the outside world would think of the massacre. They had one answer: 'The whole world will weep with the people of China.'

Chong, previously remote, was friendly to Jilly. He called to warn her it was already dangerous to wear a black armband.

'Be careful what you say, and whom you talk to. Lao Wang, the librarian, is an informer. If food runs short, you must eat with us. The British and American governments must round up the children of our leaders who are studying abroad and threaten to kill them unless the government gives in.'

'But we do not take hostages,' said Jilly.

'You must arrest them, then, and hold them till our government is crushed.'

'But in Britain we only arrest people who have broken the law,' said Jilly.

'Our leaders have broken Chinese law!' said Chong. 'Except,' he added mournfully, 'we have no law. You must use your influence with the British government.'

'But I haven't any influence.'

'People like you, from democratic countries, cannot imagine a tragedy like ours. You must tell your government, tell the world. But do not identify us. Everywhere there are informers. Many workers on campus are secret police. This afternoon there is a meeting. You must attend.'

At the meeting Mr Da was accompanied by Zhang, senior even to Chong. Zhang was interpreter for the day. Jilly realized with a jump how deeply Zhang was locked into the Chinese system of information and counterinformation.

'We are grateful for your decision to remain and to continue working,' said Zhang. 'Classes will resume this afternoon.'

'Do you think the students are in the mood for lessons?' asked Ben quietly.

'You must do the best you can.'

'Is it true soldiers are expected on campus?'

'Not this campus, only where dissidence is more serious. The safety of all foreigners is guaranteed. If the soldiers do come, we shall take you all away by car in advance. We promise to get all foreign teachers safely home.'

'And if there is civil war?'

'There will be no civil war. The rebellion is being contained.'

'Are planes flying?'

'At the moment we do not know that.'

'So how do we get home?'

Beaming, Mr Da said through Zhang that the Russians, Francine and Jilly could go home by train.

'And Mr Fox. Why is he not here?' said Zhang.

'He's disappeared.'

'I take you with me to Moscow and put you on train to Berlin,' said Irina kindly to Francine and Jilly.

'By the way,' said Mr Da, suddenly in English, 'you are very kindhearted, but it is not necessary to shelter Chinese student.'

Jilly felt a fool. The others looked sheepish.

'None of our student is missing,' said Da firmly.

'One of mine is,' said Francine.

'Two of mine,' said Tanya.

'One of mine is dead,' said Alice.

Zhang took over. 'We are looking urgently for any who are not on campus. They will be found. If food runs out in the shops, you may eat in the canteen, but remember the canteen has limited storage facilities.'

That afternoon Ben and Gloria were whisked away in an Australian Embassy car which took them to the waiting rescue plane. Gloria protested at leaving her possessions behind. Jilly hurriedly packed a holdall with summer clothes and a sponge-bag.

Soldiers invaded more important campuses and shot a few rebel students. Others were taken to jail. Bruce said he had managed to contact Hannah and reassure her. She had burst into tears on hearing that Fox was still missing. Jilly would have liked to visit Zhang but understood this might be compromising for the Professor. Jilly gave her hairdryer to Ming, who was overwhelmed. Helicopters still kept up surveillance but the shooting was now intermittent. A Chinese man in the city had been seen wearing a scarlet batwing leather jacket. Everyone said that Fox had been shot dead in the street.

An open American rescue truck arrived to take American nationals to their Embassy. Bruce took it and persuaded the driver to let Jilly hitch a ride to the British Embassy nearby. Jilly ran to pick up her bag and small cheap camera, leaving behind her books, tapes, radio and warm clothes.

'I feel like a refugee,' she said.

'That's because you *are* a refugee,' said Bruce.

'Not really. A refugee is somebody who has to leave their own home in a hurry. I'm leaving a foreign country for my own home.'

'China was my home for three years,' said Bruce, 'but I was always hopelessly American. Had to leave my computer behind, but I've got my discs. We're still alive.'

'My God,' said Jilly. 'Where's Alice? We must go back for her.'

Bruce tried to persuade the driver to return. They were three miles from campus, halfway to their destination.

But the driver, making his way through tanks, strolling soldiers and burned-out buses and lorries, expecting any minute to be shot at, dodging a Molotov cocktail, wouldn't hear of it.

'Good ole US cavalry,' said Bruce, an arm round Jilly. 'What are you doing with that camera on your wrist? People are being shot just for carrying them.' He snatched it off her hand and flung it to the back of the open truck.

'I suppose this is goodbye,' said Jilly, 'you to your Embassy, I to mine.' But the driver said it was too late to go to the Embassy. The truck pulled up at the Beijing–Toronto hotel on Chang'An Avenue, not far from the Square. Notices in English said it was forbidden to take photographs. Most of the passengers were American students, collected from all over the city. They complained they were low-budget travellers – 'although we come from nice families' – and couldn't afford posh hotels. By crowding six to a room, they reduced the cost per head. Appalled, they watched indiscriminate bloodshed on the hotel's satellite TV news. Kate Adie appeared on screen and spoke of horrors: she had been to a hospital. There were guns on the screen and shots in the street outside. Jilly felt she was taking part in some surreal thriller movie.

Bruce and Jilly shared a bed, three American girls slept in the other and a young American man insisted on sleeping on the floor. Phones rang all night. 'Daddy,' said one of the young women, 'up to now we've been well-behaved little North Carolina girls, but I'm beginning to crack. I'm scared. There's *shooting* going on out there. The Embassy say they can't do anything. Why don't they come in and get us? Do you really think you can send in a jet? That would be wonderful, daddy. Oh daddy, I do love you. I just hope I see you again. There's no public transport and hardly any taxis and it's nearly an hour to the airport. There's so much I want to do before I die!' The night was spent calling and being called. Those on the phone irritably insisted their calls were *important* and wanted the TV turned down, while the others grumbled they were hogging. Bruce got through to Hannah. Jilly got through to Rosalind.

Next morning there were three bullet holes in the window of the room next to theirs. Jilly rang the British Embassy but they were under siege because the government suspected they were harbouring a cameraman. Shooting continued in the streets and Jilly was worried her money would run out. Fortunately she had just been paid. She had forgotten to pack any clean underwear. For that brief spell she and Bruce were a couple, exchanging life-stories.

Bruce said, 'I wish we'd met when we were younger. Now it's too late.

'Yes,' said Jilly. She felt inhibited about asking him whether we would stay with Hannah or whether Hannah would want to stay with him. She was curious as to whether Bruce had been unfaithful to Hannah before, though she gathered from Hannah that he had been unfaithful to his first wife with Hannah. Perhaps Bruce was merely a sexual opportunist. If he had taken advantage of Jilly, she had been a willing accomplice. 'Bed and beddings.' Did any of it matter, compared to the tragedy of China? Bruce answered her unspoken question.

'There's Reuben, you see.'

Jilly was silent. Then she said, 'Do you think we'll ever get out of here?' She was getting worried about her bill.

'Surely,' said Bruce, squeezing her hand. 'And we're still alive!'

A doomed romance, thought Jilly. For a brief moment she wished Hannah dead. She smiled bravely at Bruce. I'm savouring the moment, she told herself. Could this be love? It was certainly an adventure. She felt reckless, energy surging through her veins. Because the room was shared by so many people, privacy was impossible.

'Did you know that Chinese has no word for privacy?' she said to Bruce.

'We had one lovely private time,' he whispered. 'You're a wonderful woman. Terrific. You're great.'

'You too,' she whispered back.

After two nights an American Embassy bus arrived to take them to the airport where a charter was off to Atlanta. The streets had become quiet. Jilly was offered a place on the plane but finding that British Airways had a plane leaving that afternoon she said goodbye to Bruce with one long kiss and booked a flight to Heathrow. At the airport café she was delighted to see Alice, who joined her fellow-Americans, and Fox. Everybody was tense, afraid the soldiers might arrive and start shooting up the airport.

'They're taking pot shots at everything,' said Jilly. 'We saw it on TV at the hotel. Blood everywhere.'

Fox and Jilly hugged each other.

'I thought you were dead!' cried Jilly.

'Me? I'm the proverbial bad penny,' said Fox.

'What happened to your red jacket?'

'How do you think I bribed a taxi?'

'Oh. What about your camcorder?'

'That was confiscated. A couple of French TV journalists had their equipment smashed and they haven't been seen since. But they let me go. We got off lightly.'

'How did Alice get to the airport?'

'She was rescued by missionaries,' said Fox. 'She's one of them, under cover.'

'Not very secret about it, though, is she? Talking of secrets, Fox, do tell: what is your Christian name?'

'It's Ethelbert,' groaned Fox.

'Did you really go to Oxford?'

'Oh yes.'

'And Mossad? BOSS?'

'I may have stretched things a little,' admitted Fox.

Fox had claimed to be a freedom fighter. The word 'freedom', thought Jilly, has acquired several new dimensions for me after living through this... e.e.cummings, was it? 'Freedom is a breakfast food'. If capitalism had some pains, communism offered few pleasures. Democracy as practised in Britain had its shortcomings, but to the woman sitting nervously in Beijing international airport it had become a precious jewel, dangling just out of her reach. She hoped desperately that she would safely board that plane, with its British crew, and that she was not about to die in a hail of Chinese bullets.

After a wait of several hours, she and Fox stepped on to the aircraft. The relief was enormous. She felt like a piece of elastic that had been stretched to breaking point. She had a massive headache and nausea. Having worn the same knickers for three days, she feared she stank. Jilly burst into tears and sobbed for half an hour. The sympathetic stewardess plied her with fresh tissues. Jilly grieved for Xiao Xu, for Ming's brother, for her son-in-law Charles (she learned later that he had neglected to take his medication), for the dead youngsters, the bereaved parents, the whole sorry mess. But she had survived and matured. Her one-night stand with Bruce had been sweet and harmed nobody. She missed Abigail, but knew it was unlikely she would ever see either Bruce or Abigail again. In the modern world, with distances so vast and travel so costly although easy, relationships were likely to be transitory and long-term commitment rare. Jilly unbuckled her seatbelt and relaxed as the plane sped Westward across China towards the Himalayas.

Ming's brother was never heard of again. Mei Ling was arrested for organizing a demonstration and spent five years in prison without trial. Children once more fly their kites in TienAnMen Square.

Hong Kong, where the massacre – now renamed 'the incident' – was commemorated by candlelight vigil every June 4 while vigils were permitted, has been returned to Chinese rule. Zhang does not write.

In Jinan, on the Yellow River, heavy goods traffic plies across the suspension bridge, eighth longest in the world, designed by a woman engineer. A peasant farmer crosses on his bicycle, wobbling, for he rides slowly. He wears a blue cotton jacket, a Mao cap and green cotton trousers, with cotton shoes. On a string he leads a huge black sow, whose enormous ears, fringed with coarse white hair, flap loose, whose multimammaries sway and judder as she waddles sedately along, engorged with milk. The farmer cannot read. He has a colour television set, but as it talks to him only in Mandarin and not his own dialect, he does not follow very much. News on Chinese television avoids controversy. Its standard fare is natural disaster: fire, flood, earthquake, punctuated by Disney movies dubbed into Mandarin. The farmer knows only vaguely that Beijing exists. He has never heard of TienAnMen Square. A butterfly flaps its wings and climates change. Slowly.

VALERIE GROSVENOR MYER won a state scholarship and took first-class honours in English literature at Newnham College, Cambridge, where she was supervised by F R Leavis and Queenie Leavis.

A sometime associate of Lucy Cavendish College, Cambridge, she has taught literature to students at Cambridge, in Beijing and in Freetown, Sierra Leone.

In 1989 she escaped from China under gunfire after the TienAnMen Square massacre, having sheltered students in her campus flat. In 1983 she chaired the Sterne session of the Canadian Association for Eighteenth Century Studies at the University of St John, New Brunswick, and has lectured in Canada, USA and France.

She has adjudicated poetry competitions, taught creative writing and made broadcasts in China, Australia and at home. Valerie has worked as a literary editor and contributed short stories, poems, essays and reviews to over fifty journals.

She reviews theatre for *The Stage* and books for the academic journal *Notes and Queries*. Her play *Nitty Gritty* has been twice produced and her novel *Culture Shock*, a deconstructed academic fantasy, was selected as one of the *Observer*'s Books of the Year 1988.